STAR THROWER

There was nothing that Jessie could do to stop the outlaw from drawing. She bent down and kept running, glancing back to see where Coulter was. He'd seen Cottle, too, and had changed his course to veer toward the house.

Then, before Cottle could level the heavy revolver, she saw a streak of bright steel flashing through the air, catching the red rays of the dropping sun. Before she could release the sigh of relief that formed in her throat, the streaking steel disk of the *shuriken* had reached its mark. It sliced into Cottle's throat, bringing a bright spurt of arterial blood.

As Cottle fell sprawling, his pistol falling to the ground from nerveless fingers, Verdis burst through the door. He was bringing up his revolver as he emerged from the opening, his head swiveling as he looked for a target, but a second flash of bright steel was already on its way. The razor-edged *shuriken* caught Verdis in the outer corner of his eye socket . . .

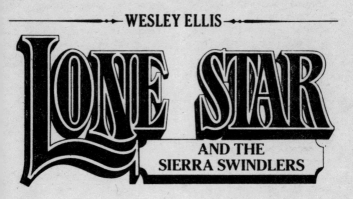

→← WESLEY ELLIS →←

LONE STAR

AND THE
SIERRA SWINDLERS

A JOVE BOOK

LONE STAR AND THE SIERRA SWINDLERS

A Jove Book/published by arrangement with
the author

PRINTING HISTORY
Jove edition/March 1987

ISBN: 0-515-08908-7

★

Chapter 1

Jessie touched Sun's reins lightly as they neared the top of the gentle upslope. Though the big palomino had been galloping now for almost two miles, Sun still breathed easily as he slowed his headlong gait, and the snarls and yowls that were coming from the other side of the slope's crest did not bother him.

As the palomino topped the rise and the land ahead fell away below her, Jessie saw the source of the shots that had been brought to her by the light late-afternoon breeze and had interrupted what was supposed to have been a leisurely afternoon outing for her and Sun, the sounds that had caused her to nudge Sun into his gallop.

A half-mile ahead, plainly visible now, a dozen gaunt-bellied prairie wolves were circling around the perimeter of a dished-out hollow. The wolves avoided the three of their number that were sprawled dead on the prairie, their attention concentrated on the half-dozen steers that milled around in the dimple that the hollow made in the prairie.

At the lowest spot of the big shallow depression, the steers were blatting and lurching, constantly upsetting the lone cowhand, snapping at him and his riderless horse. The horse, its threshing legs tangled up in its saddle gear, was rearing and pawing the ground while the Circle Star's cowhand fought to control the feisty bronco and at the same

1

time untangle the whipping leathers from the horse's constantly moving hooves.

Jessie did not need anyone to tell her what had happened after she recognized the cowhand who was in trouble. She nudged Sun's flanks with her boot heels and the palomino spurted into motion again. As she galloped down the slope toward the hollow she drew her Colt, wishing that she'd brought her Winchester on what she'd intended to be just a short, enjoyable afternoon ride that would give Sun a chance to stretch his legs.

Absorbed in trying to get his saddle leathers untangled, the cowhand did not see Jessie until Sun's swift progress had brought her halfway from the crest of the ridge to the hollow. He glanced up, and freed a hand from the tangled harness long enough to wave it in a circle at the wolves. The predators did not seem disturbed by Jessie's approach, but continued to run around the hollow's rim.

Now and then one of the boldest would make a sudden dash down into the hollow, trying to reach the legs of one of the steers to administer the hamstringing snap of its slavering jaws that would render its quarry helpless. It was not until Jessie came almost within the Colt's range that the wolves began to act disturbed. Two of them started running, but the majority of the pack continued their attacks.

Even Jessie's first shot did not stop the predators, though one of them dropped and lay twitching on the prairie grass. The second report from the Colt was followed by a sudden yelp of pain from one of the pack, which disturbed the attacking beasts, and slowed their circling. Then, when Jessie's third well-aimed slug dropped another wolf, the leader of the pack stopped its circling, and the others stopped circling also and came up to their commander.

For a moment the wolves milled restlessly, and Jessie brought down still another of them. This time her shot had an effect that exceeded the dropping of a single member of the pack. With high-pitched yelps, the leader of the wolf

2

pack streaked away from the depression. Jessie triggered off the last round left in the Colt's cylinder, and the remaining animals lost no time in following their leader. The predators were running fast, and in only a few moments were out of range of Jessie's Colt, even if she'd had any more ammunition for her weapon.

By the time Jessie reined Sun in at the edge of the scooped-out hollow, the wolf pack was in full flight, strung out in a long straggling line as they followed their leader out of danger.

"I'm sure glad to see you, Miss Jessie," the young cowhand said, letting his tangled saddle gear drop and taking off his wide-brimmed Stetson. He glanced around, frowning, and went on, "Nobody ever said anything about there being wolves on the Circle Star, so I wasn't looking for a pack of 'em to jump me."

"Usually there aren't any," Jessie said. "But now and then a pack that's been driven off from one of the other ranches will settle in here. I hadn't heard any of the men mention seeing them, though."

"Well, that bunch sure caught me with my britches down, if you'll excuse me saying it that way."

"I've heard the expression before," Jessie said dryly.

"I guess I sorta made a mess outa things, didn't I?"

"Yes, I'd say you did a pretty fair job, Tinker," Jessie agreed, her eyes traveling over the wolf and cattle carcasses.

"Well, I don't reckon I can hand out much in the way of excuses for not handling things right," Tinker admitted. "But I'm real sorry I cost you a couple of nice steers. I wouldn't blame you if you was to tell me to turn in my time and go look for a job someplace else."

"I'm not going to tell you that," Jessie replied. "But if the foreman fires you, I won't do anything to stop him. I suppose it was his idea to send you out by yourself?"

"Well—" Tinker stopped, frowning. "He told me to ride out this way and look for strays, and if I found any to drive

3

'em back to the main herd. I seen these stragglers, but before I had much of a chance to herd 'em into a bunch my girth cinch busted and throwed me. Then when I got up and started trying to fix my gear, them wolves was right on top of the steers and I didn't quite know what to do."

"You explain that when you get back, and see what he says then," Jessie suggested. "You might get off light this time." Privately, she resolved to have a quiet chat with the foreman and suggest that it wasn't the best idea to send a green hand out alone. She went on, "Now, do you need any help, or can you get your horse saddled again and finish driving these steers back to the main herd?"

"Oh, I can take care of cleaning up my own mess, Miss Jessie," Tinker answered. "I'll have 'em herded over to the main bunch and be back at the bunkhouse in time for supper."

"Then I'll ride on." Jessie nodded.

She touched Sun's flank with the toe of her boot and the palomino responded. Riding on, enjoying the freshening breeze that was springing up as the day neared its close, she let Sun set his own gait until they reached the last rise and she saw the buildings and corrals of the Circle Star breaking the level surface of the seemingly endless Southwest Texas prairie. Sun nickered and Jessie leaned forward in her saddle to pat the palomino's shoulder.

"You've had your run," Jessie told the horse as she settled back into the saddle. "We'll take it easy the rest of the way, and by the time we get to the corral you'll be cool and calm and ready for supper."

Sun tossed his head as though to signify he'd understood her words perfectly, as perhaps he had. The communication between Jessie and the golden stallion did not depend on words alone. Because of the mysterious understanding that often exists between favored horses and their human masters, Jessie hadn't really needed to speak. Sun knew the terrain of the Circle Star as well as Jessie did herself, and she was sure the highly intelligent animal realized that their afternoon outing had come to an end.

As they drew closer to the big stone main house, which was set a little apart from the bunkhouse and cookshack, the barns, and the other outbuildings, Jessie saw Ki come out of the cookshack and start toward the main house. Ki saw Jessie at about the same time she saw him, and he changed his course, heading for the small corral that stood a bit apart from the bigger corral used by the hands for their working animals. He opened the gate and waited for Jessie to ride in, then joined her as she swung out of her saddle.

"Do you want me to give you a hand getting Sun's saddle off?" he asked.

"Oh, I'll do it myself," Jessie said, her hands already on the cincha strap. She finished pulling the strap free and let the weight of the girth drag it from the ring. Then, as she stepped away from Sun's side, she went on, "But you can swing it over the fence rail, if you'd like. I think I'll go out again in the morning and watch the sunrise."

"You're enjoying resting, aren't you?" Ki asked.

"Of course. After all the busy years we spent before wiping out the cartel, this kind of peaceful life is something I can really enjoy." Then a frown rippled over Jessie's perfect oval face and she went on, "I only wish Alex was here to share it."

Alex Starbuck, Jessie's father, had been the creator of the huge Circle Star ranch, which spread over most of three West Texas counties and covered an area greater than some of the small nations of Europe. Of all the properties she'd inherited after Alex's murder by the hired killers of the vicious, foreign-based cartel he'd dedicated himself to abolishing, Jessie valued the Circle Star the most.

During the years she'd spent carrying out the job her father had started, Jessie had been able to spend only a limited amount of time at the ranch. She and Ki, who served her as he'd served Alex, with boundless devotion and dedication, had spent most of their time fighting the cartel. Now, with the cartel smashed and its sinister power destroyed, Jessie was able to devote all her time to the seemingly endless details of supervising the vast industrial empire that Alex had created during his lifetime and that was now her responsibility.

She and Ki still found it necessary to spend a good part of their time away from the Circle Star. The Starbuck properties were sprawled over the face of the United States. They included mines in California and Utah, Arizona and New Mexico; vast agricultural acreage in California and the Upper Midwest; timberlands in the Pacific Northwest as well as in the Great Lakes region. In addition to these, there were foundries and shipyards on the West Coast; banking and brokerage interests in Los Angeles, San Francisco, Chicago, Pittsburgh, Boston, and New York.

Because no man who'd attained Alex's stature in the world of business and finance could escape involvement in politics, Jessie found an occasional visit to Washington necessary. There she was frequently the guest of President and Mrs. Hayes at the White House, and even more often her hosts were members of the Senate from states where the Starbuck interests were most highly concentrated.

No matter where she'd traveled, Ki had been with her, bound by the invisible strings of the loyalty he'd given Alex for having taken him in as a youth. The same strings had kept him tied to Jessie, for Ki's own Japanese family had banished him from its councils because of the stubborn racial prejudice its elders held against his half-Japanese, half-American parentage. Before he'd encountered Alex, Ki had wandered the Orient, but his wanderings through those strange, sealed, violent lands had resulted in one boon: a long period of study at the dojo of the master warrior Hirata, where he'd become totally adept in the Oriental martial arts.

It was small wonder, then, that Jessie valued above all else the time she could spend on the Circle Star. The isolation of the big cattle spread had become a blessing and a

6

boon. She was as grateful for the ranch now after the cartel's demise as she had been during the years when she and Ki were the targets of its vicious operatives trying to smash the Starbuck industrial empire.

"There's a new bag of mail in the study," Ki remarked as he and Jessie started walking toward the main house. "Gimpy took time from the cookshack to ride up to the railroad—he was looking for some fresh vegetables to come in—and he picked up the mail while he was there."

"Opening the mailbag doesn't bother me any more." Jessie smiled as she went into the main house. "At least I know that all it will have in it is the business reports, instead of some piece of information that will lead to a fight against the cartel."

"Let's just be glad that we don't have to worry about the cartel any longer," Ki remarked as he followed Jessie into the big room that formed the core and heart of the Circle Star's main house.

More than any other feature of the ranch, this room held for Jessie the strongest memories of her father, as well as the only real reminder she had of the mother who'd died giving birth to her. Life-sized, full-length portraits of Alex and her mother adorned the wall at each end of the almost-square, high-ceilinged chamber.

All the furniture had been chosen by Alex: deep leather-upholstered armchairs and an oversized divan, the big roll-top desk that Alex had bought secondhand when he opened the little Oriental arts curio shop in San Francisco that had been his first business venture. There were tables scattered here and there, and a priceless embroidered Oriental screen shielded one corner where a small, richly enameled stand held a miniature spirit burner, copper kettle, and brown-glazed teapot.

Ki was the most frequent user of the tea-brewing utensils, often when the discussions he and Jessie held about the administration of the Starbuck business enterprises lasted well into the early-morning hours. When they entered the big room this time, though, Ki waited until Jessie had settled into the big leather-upholstered easy chair that had been Alex's favorite and still held a faint, ghostly fragrance of his cherry-flavored pipe tobacco. Then Ki took the chair nearest Jessie and settled back while he waited for her to open the mailbag.

"There's hardly anything here this time," Jessie commented as she upended the bag over the table beside her chair and a half-dozen envelopes dropped onto the tabletop. "A few letters and that overdue report from Stratton on the timber operations up in Oregon."

As Jessie spoke, she picked up one of the envelopes, tore it open, scanned it quickly, and went on, "And the only thing that looks like it needs immediate attention is this telegram from Frank Allison in San Francisco."

"Don't tell me that someone's suing you, or threatening to," Ki said. "If that's the case, it probably means a trip to the West Coast."

"It's just the opposite," Jessie replied as she handed the yellow flimsy to Ki. "Frank's recommending that I sue somebody who's using the Starbuck name to promote what he says can only be a gold-mining swindle."

"Well, it wouldn't be the first time that's happened," Ki commented as he read the message. "I'm sure you haven't forgotten the woman from the cartel who posed as you a while back and created quite a good deal of mischief."

"Blanche Gregory." Jessie nodded. "Yes, I remember her very well, Ki, and how much trouble we had running her to earth. This doesn't seem to be the same kind of thing at all, but if somebody's using my name to promote any kind of swindle or cheat, I'd certainly want to stop it."

"Suppose we wait until we get the letter that Allison says is on the way," Ki suggested. "It'll be here in a few days. Then, after you see exactly what's happening, we can do whatever's necessary."

"I suppose that is the best thing," Jessie agreed. "A few

days shouldn't make that much difference. We'll wait, then."

Actually, only three days passed before Jessie received the promised letter. It came in a fat envelope, containing not only a letter from Frank Allison, but full pages of the Los Angeles *Express* and the San Francisco *Chronicle*. The newspaper clippings were identical advertisements. In glaring oversized type, they read:

CHANCE OF A LIFETIME!
CASH IN ON GOLD FROM A MINING CLAIM
IN THE HIGH SIERRAS ORIGINALLY
DEVELOPED BY THE FAMOUS
ALEX STARBUCK!
THIS CAN MAKE YOU RICH!
FOR DETAILS WRITE TO *GOLD MINES,
SIERRA CITY, CALIFORNIA.*
WRITE OR COME UP TODAY!
FREE ACCOMMODATIONS IN SIERRA CITY!
DON'T MISS OUT ON
THIS CHANCE FOR WEALTH!

"Whoever wrote this advertisement certainly wasn't bashful about making claims," Jessie remarked wryly. "And I don't mean the kind of claims prospectors file."

"I have to agree with you." Ki nodded after he'd looked at the papers. "What did Frank Allison say in his letter?"

"Just that the Sierra City mentioned in the advertisement is a real place. And Frank looked up the land Sierra City seems to be on. It's in the inventory of Alex's estate, even though I don't remember it. Frank says it's listed along with other undeveloped property in a section of the will that he calls 'miscellaneous assets.'"

"Then it's your land we're talking about." Ki frowned. "I have the same trouble you do, though, Jessie. I don't

9

recall any details about the property, except that Alex looked at and even bought options on several parcels of land before he finally decided to settle down here on the Circle Star."

"That would explain it, of course," Jessie said thoughtfully. "I didn't pay much attention to the miscellaneous list when I was trying to get acquainted with Alex's business ventures after his death. They took up all my time that wasn't devoted to fighting the cartel, and to this day I haven't checked out all the holdings that are on the miscellaneous list."

"I do remember what Alex told me about his trip to Sierra City, even though I didn't visit it with him," Ki went on. "He said the place sits on top of a mountain ridge in the middle of the Sierra Nevadas, just inside the state line between California and Nevada."

"How big a town is it?"

"I haven't any idea, Jessie. But there are so few people who actually live in the Sierras that I suppose any place with more than a half-dozen houses automatically becomes a town."

"And are there any gold diggings near this Sierra City?"

"I suppose there must be some," Ki replied thoughtfully.

"I'd be surprised if there weren't," Jessie said. "From what I've heard, there are traces of gold all over the Sierra Nevadas."

"Sierra City isn't inside the placer mining belt, though," Ki reminded her. "It's too high up. Any gold from around there would have to be mined, not panned the way they do in the streams lower down."

"Well, I suppose the only way to get to the bottom of this is to go out to California, see exactly what's going on, find out who's putting these ads in the papers, and put a stop to it," Jessie said. "I certainly don't want to see the Starbuck name attached to any swindles."

"When do you want to leave?" Ki asked.

"It'd put us in too much of a rush to leave tomorrow,"

10

she said, frowning. "Besides that, if we put off leaving until the day after tomorrow, we'll be able to get the new train the Southern Pacific's been bragging about, the one with Mr. Pullman's sleeping cars on it. At least we won't have to sit up at night during the trip."

"Whatever you say, Jessie," Ki agreed. "I'll be ready."

★

Chapter 2

"It seems to me that we've been waiting here a long time for the train to start," Jessie observed, peering out the window of the Pullman coach into the blackness of the night. "But I suppose it does take quite a while to make the connections that are necessary."

"We're just not familiar with this train," Ki said. "This is the first time we've taken this new fast mail express. The old train's a lot slower."

"Your friend Ki is right about that, ma'am," Avery Coulter said from his seat across the aisle from Jessie and Ki.

When Jessie and Ki had changed trains in Los Angeles, they'd found themselves and Coulter the only passengers in the extra-fare Pullman coach. Coulter had gotten on the train just a few moments before it pulled out of the depot, and aside from a polite nod as he settled into his seat he'd had nothing to say. Immediately after the train left the depot he'd taken several sheaves of paper from his briefcase and had devoted all his attention to them.

Ki had looked out the window for a few moments now and then before darkness hid the view, and then had leaned his head back against the green-plush headrest and dozed. When Jessie had grown bored with gazing out the window during the slow uphill haul as the train chugged up the rising flanks of the Tehachapi Mountains, she'd followed

Ki's example and dozed, but during her wakeful moments she'd glanced at the new passenger a few times.

He was a young man, conservatively dressed in a standard three-piece suit from a fairly skillful tailor. He'd put his gray derby hat on the rack above his seat, revealing a full head of neatly trimmed hair too dark to be blond and too light to be brown. His features were regular, nothing about them distinguishing him from the other young, aggressive businessmen who'd lately been flocking to Southern California as its growing population began hinting that at some future date it might rival the more settled northern area based in San Francisco.

Jessie had placed the man early on as a traveling salesman of some sort, and wondered idly what the figures that he found so engrossing signified, but eventually she, too, had taken refuge in short naps.

Not until the conductor came through to light the gaslight ceiling lamps did the young man fold his papers and restore them to his briefcase. Then he'd turned and spoken across the aisle to Jessie.

"I'm afraid I haven't been very good company," he'd said. "But I needed to catch up on my orders while the details were still fresh in my mind. But let me introduce myself."

He'd taken a business card from his vest pocket and passed it across the aisle to Jessie. It read: "Avery Coulter, Factory Representative, Pace Furniture Company."

"I'd placed you as a traveling man when I first saw you," Jessie had said. "My name's Jessica Starbuck. I'd introduce you to Ki, who's my—well, I guess you'd say aide as well as friend, but as you can see, he's asleep."

"They'll make up the berths in the car here when we stop at the top of the mountains, before we start down the Loop," Coulter said. "Then we can join Ki in sleeping."

Jessie frowned as there was a grinding squeal from the front of the train and the Pullman bucked, then slowed.

14

She tried to peer out the window, but all she could see was blackness. She said, "I don't see any reason for stopping here."

"We're at the foot of the Tehachapis," Coulter told her. "This is where they couple on a second locomotive to get us up and down those steep grades in the Loop."

"Then how far are we from Tehachapi?" Jessie asked.

"About three hours. It's a pretty good haul from the bottom of the grade," Avery said.

As he spoke, the car lurched and started moving again. Ki broke into the conversation. "You said they were putting on another engine. Is the grade that steep?"

"It's steeper going down than going up," Coulter replied. "We'll need the booster engine to slow us up as we go down the Loop. After that, it's a real smooth ride to the Bay."

"It sounds like you know this railroad chapter and verse," Jessie remarked. "You must travel on it a lot."

"More than I like to think about. But it all goes with my line of business, so I guess—" Coulter broke off as the vestibule door opened and the conductor entered the coach.

"Have you seen anybody pass through this car?" the trainman asked, looking from Coulter to Jessie to Ki.

Jessie shook her head. "No. Is something wrong?"

"I don't want you to get any ideas that'll upset you, Miss Starbuck," the conductor replied, "but the extra brakemen who were supposed to be waiting at the signal shanty didn't get there for some reason. The engineer on the booster locomotive figures they'll be waiting at the top of the grade, and we don't really need them until then."

"I know enough about railroad cars to give you a hand, if you need me," Ki volunteered. "At least, I can get up on top of a car and turn a brake wheel."

"Thanks all the same, but it's the engine crew's problem, and they say they can handle the train all right without the two extra brakies," the conductor replied. "But I'd better make up your berths now, because I might have to help on the brakes myself if those extra men don't show up at the top of the grade."

"Whatever you say." Ki nodded. "But if you need help, be sure to let me know."

"Thanks, I will," the trainman replied. "Now, don't bother to move out of where you're sitting. The car's so close to being empty, I can make up the berths on some of the other seats."

Jessie, Ki, and Coulter sat quiet, watching while the trainman lowered the bulging domes of the upper berths on three of the vacant seats and swiftly converted the seats themselves to provide the lowers. The job was completed in a few minutes, then the trainman said, "You folks can turn in whenever you feel like it. Now, I'd better get moving, because we'll be at the top of the grade in just a few minutes more."

Even to those in the Pullman coach it was obvious when the train reached the summit of the mountains and started down the grade. For several minutes they'd been moving slower and slower, until the train was barely moving. It inched along for what seemed to be a very long time, then came to a stop. They heard shouts from outside and Jessie raised the window shade to get a better view. When she peered out into the darkness she saw lanterns bobbing, and the dark silhouettes of men walking about on the right-of-way.

"I guess everything's all right," she said. "Maybe the men they were short of showed up, because all of them out there are starting to get back on board."

With a clashing of couplings, the train jerked, then settled down to a slow crawl as it began moving again. Looking out once more, Jessie saw there were no more moving forms or lanterns on the right-of-way. Satisfied, she pulled the shade down.

Gradually the noises of the starting train merged into a rhythmic click-clacking as it gained speed. Jessie leaned back and let her head fall back against the plush headrest. She'd just closed her eyes and was considering going to the greater comfort of her berth when feet clattered to the floor across the aisle. She glanced around and saw that Coulter had gotten to his feet.

"Don't be alarmed," he said when he saw her looking at him. "But I've got a hunch that we're not out of the woods yet. We're picking up speed a lot faster than we're supposed to on this downgrade."

For the first time Jessie noticed that the railroad coach was beginning to sway from side to side as it sped down the steep grade. In the seat beside her, Ki straightened up and leaned across her to pull the shade away from the window and peer out.

"My guess is that he's right, Jessie," he said. "Let's go along with Coulter."

By the time they caught up with the young drummer he was near the end of the car.

"Now, don't jump to any conclusions," Coulter told them. "We'll find out soon enough if there's trouble."

They reached the door at the back and stepped out onto the vestibule. The conductor was on the stubby platform, leaning out, looking toward the engine.

"We're still in trouble, aren't we?" Jessie asked.

"We sure shouldn't be moving this fast on such a steep downgrade," the conductor replied. "I'm going to walk through the cars up to the engine and tell that fool engineer to put the brakes on sooner than he usually does, so we'll stop at the foot of the grade," the conductor said. "But that's not something for you to worry about, Miss Starbuck. Just go back to your seat and you'll be all right."

"Can I help?" Ki asked.

"I'd be glad to give you a hand, too," Coulter offered.

"Not right now," the trainman said. "But thanks all the same. Now, I'd better go see what I can find out."

The conductor stepped through the back door of the coach and walked swiftly down the aisle and into the next

17

car. He'd been out of sight less than a minute when a shot sounded from somewhere at the front of the train. Ki glanced at Jessie, a question in his eyes.

"Yes," she said. "It sounds like the conductor might be needing a little help."

Another pair of shots, widely spaced, sounded while Jessie was still speaking. Ki needed nothing more. He leaped to his feet and started toward the door through which the conductor had gone. Jessie bent forward and pulled her valise from beneath her seat. She had opened it and was reaching in for her Colt when she got a glimpse of movement across the aisle. Looking around, she saw that Coulter was taking a businesslike Smith & Wesson from his own handgrip.

"You check the back, then come forward," Jessie said. "I'll follow Ki. Now that somebody's started shooting, we'll know what to do."

She did not wait for Coulter to acknowledge her command, but started at once to the door Ki had gone through at the front of the coach. Before she left the car she glanced over her shoulder and saw the young drummer hurrying down the aisle toward the back of the coach. Then she heard the vestibule door open, and the cool night breeze was sweeping in. The full moon that had come up made the night almost daylight-bright.

Just as Jessie stepped out onto the vestibule, Ki swung down from the top of the coach. He did not swing easily, as was his habit, but gave most of his attention to helping the wounded conductor down the laderlike steps attached to the sides of the coach.

"You got here just in time," he said, his voice as cool as though he were making a remark about the weather. "Our friend the conductor found out what's wrong, all right. The train's being held up by a bunch of outlaws!"

Jessie asked no questions and made no comments on Ki's statement. Instead, she said calmly, "Stay on the lad-

18

der and lower his feet. I'll pull him onto the vestibule, then we can take him inside the coach."

On the steep downgrade, the train was still picking up speed. It was swaying and jolting now as it raced through the darkness, but in spite of the unpredictable sidewise swings of the speeding car Jessie managed to grab the conductor's legs. For a moment the trainman resisted her unfamiliar touch, then he relaxed as he realized that the hands holding him were those of helpers, not enemies. After that, Jessie and Ki had very little trouble in lowering the semiconscious conductor to the vestibule platform.

By the time Ki swung off the ladder and joined Jessie, shots were no longer sounding. The only noises that broke the night were the rushing whistle of the wind as it whipped around the corners of the speeding coach, the creaks of the layered wooden sides of the railroad car itself, and an occasional distant shout. Even these faded and became only semiaudible after Jessie and Ki had carried the conductor into the coach and laid him down on a seat. He stirred after a moment and raised his blood-streaked face to look up at Jessie.

"Outlaws," he muttered hoarsely. "Trainrobbers."

"Do you know who they are?" Jessie asked.

"No." The railroader shook his head groggily. "Know how they pull jobs like this, though."

Ki had disappeared into the lavatory at the end of the car as soon as he and Jessie had laid the conductor across the seat. He reappeared now, carrying a water-soaked towel. Jessie took the cloth and mopped the blood off the conductor's face. With the blood-soaked area cleared, she could see that the man's wound was only a bullet crease low on his temple, a surface graze that had bled a lot but had done no real damage.

Jessie resumed her questioning. "Tell us what to expect," she said. "Then maybe we'll know how to hold off the robbers."

"There's two or three gangs pulls these jobs," the conductor replied. He was recovering fast. His speech was no longer slurred and the glazed look was leaving his eyes. "They've done it more than once before now, and all of 'em work pretty much the same. They'll have three or four men—one of 'em takes over the locomotive and starts the drag moving, then pulls the loco off onto a siding."

"Are you telling me that gravity is pulling this train down the grade at the speed we're moving?" Jessie broke in to ask.

"It's a steep drop, Miss Starbuck," the trainman replied. "But if there was an engine pulling this string I'd sure know it."

Jessie nodded. "I didn't mean to interrupt you," she told the conductor. "Go ahead."

"Like I was saying, soon as the cars pick up speed, the outlaws on board go through the cars and tell the passengers to keep quiet. Then they let the cars roll downgrade—and this loop's got a steep one—and put on the brakes at the bottom. Once the drag's stopped, they grab what money the passengers are carrying and clear out the safe in the baggage coach, then get away on horses they've got waiting out in the brush away from the track."

"What're the railroad police doing while all this is going on?" Jessie asked, then added quickly, "Or the regular police, for that matter? Are there railroad detectives on this train?"

Shaking his head, the conductor replied to her last question, "None that I know about."

"You'd know if there were, wouldn't you?"

"More than likely, but I don't know all the bulls the railroad hires. I don't imagine there's any aboard, or they'd have come up to me and introduced themselves before now."

"They would have unless they're terribly inefficient," she agreed. "Or unless they're in cahoots with the robbers."

"That's not likely," the conductor answered. "The railroad police work out of division points, and it's local gangs of crooks that pull the robberies."

"You'd probably know that better than I do," Jessie told him. "It looks like we can't expect any help, then, so let's decide what we can do ourselves."

Ki broke in to ask, "How long is this Tehachapi Loop? What I'm trying to figure out is how much time we have."

"Well, the Loop's a mile, give or take a bit," the conductor replied. He paused again to gasp and shake his head as though to rid himself of pain, then went on, "As for exactly when we'll be stopping, I wish I could tell you that. But like I just said, they usually put the brakes on at the bottom of the grade."

"Wherever they stop, I'll be ready for 'em!" a new voice broke in.

Jessie, Ki, and the conductor turned as one to look toward the front end of the coach. Avery Coulter stood just inside the vestibule door. His hands were on his hips, pulling his coat open to show the gun tucked into the center of his belt. Against the white shirt the black grip of his Smith & Wesson stood out in sharp contrast. The car was beginning to sway from side to side again now as the train picked up speed on the steep downgrade, and Coulter was forced to reach out a hand to the back of the nearest seat to brace himself as the swaying became more and more pronounced.

"I got off a couple of shots," the traveling salesman said. "But I'm not sure whether or not I hit either one of those bandits that've taken over the train."

"There are two of them in the front part of the train, then?" Jessie asked.

Coulter nodded. "And by now there'll be at least one at the back of this car we're in," he replied. "For all I know, there might be another one or two in the baggage coach as well."

"There might be, at that," the conductor agreed.

21

"They'd know that's where the safe is."

"It's clear what we need to do, then," Jessie said briskly. She turned to the conductor. "As soon as you feel like moving, start walking through the train and warn the passengers not to get in our way. Tell them to lie down on the floor, so they won't get hurt when the shooting starts."

"Who's going to be shooting?" Coulter asked.

"You and I," Jessie replied quickly. "And the conductor, too, if he has a gun. Ki has his own weapons he'll be using, but they're silent."

"I've got a gun, all right," the conductor broke in. "And I'm not afraid to use it. But it's my job to keep the passengers as safe as possible, so maybe I'd better stay inside the train and do what I can to keep the passengers out of trouble."

"Just make them stay inside the coaches where they won't be in our way," Jessie said. "If we do that, we won't mistake any of them for the bandits."

By now the wheel flanges were screaming almost constantly as the railroad coach swayed from side to side, and an assortment of squeaks and groans created by the rubbing of the triple-layered wooden walls of the speeding coach as they protested the stresses placed on them were adding to the din that filled the air as the train rocketed down the grade. Jessie had to raise her voice to be heard as she turned to Coulter.

"Suppose you go with the conductor," she added. "He can tell you when you get to the middle of the train. Then go out between the cars and wait until we stop. That's when the bandits will try to get away, and when we'll have the best chance to stop them without putting the passengers in danger. Now let's all get in place without wasting any more time," Jessie said. "And be ready when the holdup gang stops the train to make their getaway."

Coulter and the conductor started walking toward the front of the coach. The train was bouncing so erratically now that they were forced to grasp the backs of the seats to keep from being thrown off their feet. Jessie watched them leave, then turned to Ki.

"I didn't put you in any specific place," she said. She had to raise her voice almost to a shout to be heard above the constant screeching of the flanged wheels as the car continued its plunge down the steep incline. "You'll know where you want to be to act most effectively."

"On top of the cars, of course," Ki replied. "But don't worry about that. I can climb to the top from the front vestibule of this car we're in and use *ninjutsu* to get up ahead to the baggage car without the outlaws seeing me."

★

Chapter 3

Knowing Ki's great skill with the *ninja* art of moving almost invisibly, Jessie nodded silently. Ki started to the front of the car and Jessie made her way to the rear. She stepped out onto the back vestibule, finding the night strangely quiet after the din that had filled the car's interior. Though the wheel flanges still shrilled as they ground against the rails, and the rattle of the coaches provided an undercurrent of sound, most of the noise made by the freewheeling train was lost in the open air.

For a moment Jessie stood on the truncated platform of the vestibule, letting her eyes adjust to the darkness. Then she moved to the side edge of the platform and swung out to grasp the rungs of the ladder that led to the top of the coach. She climbed the quivering ladder almost to the top, then stopped and drew her Colt before raising her head cautiously to look at the roof of the passenger coach before going the rest of the way.

When her head broke the roofline, Jessie saw the boot soles of one of the train robbers level with her eyes. The man was lying prone on his belly, facing the front of the train, and even in the darkness Jessie could see the glint of steel from the revolver he held in his hand. Jessie tightened her grip on the grab rail and raised her Colt just as the man turned his head, saw her, and started to swing his pistol around to fire.

In the instant that passed before the gun barked, Jessie saw the blurred glint of Ki's *shuriken* streaking through the darkness. The whirling sawtoothed edge of the circular throwing blade shed pinpoints of light before it found its mark in the outlaw's throat, a split second before he could trigger off the shot he intended for Jessie.

As the dying man's finger tightened on the trigger the revolver barked, but the weapon's muzzle was already sagging downward when it spat a burst of angry red flame. The lead kicked up a harmless spurt of dust that was swallowed by the darkness of the railroad grade while the booming report of the futile shot was half-drowned by the rumble of the speeding train.

Then the pistol dropped from the outlaw's hand and his left hand relaxed its grip on the grab rail. For a moment the outlaw's lifeless body hung poised on the car's domed edge, then the curve in the track did its work in dislodging the body. The dead man's body brushed past Jessie as it fell in a sprawl of lifeless, swinging arms and legs to lie still on the roadbed until it was hidden in the darkness after the coach passed.

Jessie could see Ki silhouetted against the streaks of light that the windows of the passenger coach ahead of him cast on the roadbed. She waved and Ki nodded in reply before turning and beginning to move toward the baggage car, the first car of the runaway train. Jessie continued her climb up the ladder until she stood on top of the swaying coach. The train was still gaining speed, moving ever faster in its headlong course down the steep, inclined curve of the Tehachapi Loop, and Jessie had some trouble holding her balance as she started moving slowly toward the front end of the car.

When she got to the front she looked at the six-foot gap between it and the rear end of the car next in the string. For a moment she stood poised to jump, then decided that caution was to be preferred to valor. Holstering her Colt, she dropped flat and climbed down the ladder to the vestibule,

26

then stepped over the foot-wide gap without trouble. As she opened the door to go in the muffled report of a distant gunshot reached her ears and she hesitated for a moment, then pushed through the door and entered the car.

A buzz of excited conversation from the half-dozen passengers who occupied the car's green seats greeted her ears. Jessie started up the aisle, but she'd taken only a step or two before one of the women passengers grabbed her wrist.

"Would you please tell us what's going on outside?" the woman asked. "That conductor told us to keep our seats and stay calm, but how's a body going to do that when there's shooting and who knows what all else going on outside!"

"Some bandits are trying to rob the train," Jessie said matter-of-factly as she stopped beside the frowning, frantic-looking woman and gently removed the hand that was still clamped around her wrist with a grip like that of an iron claw. On both sides of the aisle the other passengers swiveled around, trying to identify the source of the voices. Speaking loudly enough to be heard from one end of the car to the other, Jessie went on, "If all of you will just do what the conductor told you to, you'll be all right."

"How in tunket can anybody stay calm when they're being shot at?" the woman demanded.

"That's a very good question," Jessie replied. "But you sit right where you are and keep thinking about what the man in charge of the train told you to do, and I'm sure you'll manage somehow."

Almost before Jessie stopped speaking, a new and higher-pitched squeal of steel against steel cut through the air. The coach swayed harder, then a series of thudding crashes sounded from outside the car. The coach shivered and shook for a moment, then bucked to a stop.

"What on earth was that?" the panicked woman passenger demanded, her jaw dropping.

"I'm not sure," Jessie said calmly. "But it's a noise I've

27

heard before, and unless I'm mistaken the booster locomotive just jumped off the tracks."

Except for a loud hissing of escaping steam outside, the coach had been virtually silent while the passengers were listening to the conversation between Jessie and the frightened woman. Now cries of alarm broke out.

"All of us better run!" a man yelled from the front end of the coach. "When engines jump off the rails they're liable to blow up!"

Raising her voice, Jessie shouted, "Don't be a fool! Sit quietly right where you are! Even if the engine does blow up, you'll be safer here in the coach then you would be outside!"

"She's right!" someone spoke up at the back of the car. "If you're outside when the engine blows you might be killed!"

"Besides, there's them shots we heard," another called. "It might be there's a whole bunch of train robbers out there!"

"Just stay in the coach here," Jessie urged again, raising her voice so all the passengers could hear. "I'll go see what I can find out."

Waiting for a moment until the excited passengers had calmed down, Jessie walked on through the car, stopping once or twice to reassure an especially panicky passenger until she reached the end of the coach. She stepped quickly across the vestibule to the next car and found it deserted. Hurrying through the coach, she went through the door onto the vestibule and stepped into the open space between the passenger coach and the baggage car.

Gun in hand, Avery Coulter was standing on the baggage-car vestibule. His back was toward Jessie, and when she touched his shoulder lightly he jumped and swiveled around to face her, bringing up his pistol.

"It's all right," Jessie assured him, stepping out of the line of fire of the drummer's weapon. "There don't seem to be any more bandits in the cars I just left. Did you see where Ki went? He started up toward the front of the train, but I've lost track of him."

"He's in the baggage coach with the conductor," Coulter told her. "At least, that's where I saw him go, and that's the car where the shooting came from a minute ago. But I haven't heard any more from in there, so I guess they're all right."

"If you didn't hear any more shots, they must be," Jessie agreed.

She stepped up to the baggage-car door and pushed it open. It opened only a couple of inches, letting a stream of yellow lantern light flood the vestibule, before it thunked against something and stopped. Looking down, Jessie saw a pair of boot-clad feet lying, toes up, on the floor of the car. She could not see the legs above the knees, where the edge of the door had bumped into them. Then Ki's face appeared in the crack of the open door.

"It's all right, Jessie," he said. "I think we've wiped out the bunch that was intending to rob the train. The conductor and I surprised two of them while they were trying to open the safe in here. They're both dead now."

"That accounts for the shot I heard a minute ago, I suppose," Jessie remarked.

Ki nodded. "It was the conductor shooting. When we came in here the outlaws were trying to open the safe, and they didn't look up in time. He got one and my *shuriken* accounted for the other."

"And you're all right?" Jessie asked.

"Of course," Ki answered. "The conductor is, too. He's forgotten all about that scratch the bullet put on his face. And it's pretty plain that you're all right, too."

"So is our friend the furniture drummer," Jessie said. "He told me where you were, and he's waiting out here with me, if you'd like to join us."

"Sorry, but I can't," Ki told her. "The conductor asked me to stay in here with him. He thinks there might be some more of the gang lurking around outside."

Speaking over Jessie's shoulder, Avery told Ki, "I'll be glad to help you if you need me."

Stepping up behind Ki, the conductor said quickly, "We can hold out in here, but you'd better go back to the other passengers. You'll be a lot safer. What we got in here isn't fit for a lady to look at."

"I've seen dead men before now," Jessie told the man.

"Just the same, I'd feel better if you was to go back to the Pullman. Now that the bandits have run, you just stay in there and wait, " the trainman said.

"Wait for what?" Jessie asked.

"Till we can be sure there aren't any more of the gang hanging around."

"You know who these outlaws were who attacked us, then?"

"I can't be sure, but like I was just telling your Chinese friend in here, I got an idea they're from the Mason-Henry gang," the conductor replied. "They've pulled this same trick once before and got away with it. My hunch is they figured it was good enough for a repeat. But we won't know for sure till the sheriff gets around to take a look at the bodies."

"And I don't suppose that will be until later?"

"Likely not until late, most likely after daylight, seeing it's past midnight now," the conductor agreed. "But your bunk in the Pullman makes as good a bed as any, so you can get some rest while we wait for another engine to come up from Tehachapi. It's likely to take a while. I'll tap onto the railroad telegraph with my key soon as things calm down, but it's going to be a while before a relief train gets here."

"I suppose I might as well be sleeping, since there doesn't seem to be much I can do here." Jessie nodded. "You can call me if you need anything more."

Jessie walked back through the train, stopping long enough in the day coach to assure the nervous passengers that two of the outlaws who'd tried to rob the train were

30

dead and the others had been driven off. Then she went on to the Pullman car. The green curtains shielding Coulter's bunk were drawn, and Jessie assumed that the furniture drummer had gone to bed. She went to her own bunk, where the curtains were still agape.

Wasting no time, suddenly tired and ready to relax, Jessie drew the curtains and shielded her bunk from the aisle. She laid her holstered Colt on the mattress, tossing her clothing on top of it as she took off her skirt and blouse and thin cambric pantalettes. Then she stretched out and tried to relax, but she was still tossing restlessly, too keyed up from the night's excitement to sleep well, when she heard the soft sound of fingers brushing across the thick green curtain.

"Ki?" she whispered.

"No, ma'am." The voice she heard replying in an equally soft whisper was that of Avery Coulter. "He'll likely stay down there with the conductor till that relief engine gets here."

"Mr. Coulter?"

"Avery, if you don't mind, Miss Starbuck. I just figured you might be having as much trouble getting to sleep as I was, and I thought maybe we could help each other out."

"I'm sure I understand what you're suggesting," Jessie said. "But I'm not sure this is the time or place for it."

"We're not likely to have another chance," Coulter whispered.

"I didn't dare to let on how hard I fell for you the first time I set eyes on you," he went on, his voice growing urgent now. "But I'd sure like to tell you, if you'll give me a chance to."

Jessie lay silent for a moment, considering the drummer's proposal. For the past several months she'd been in isolation at the Circle Star, cloistered as effectively as though she'd been in a nunnery, and she was honest enough with herself to admit that Coulter's proposal appealed to her. Typically, she did not delay her decision.

31

"Go out on the back vestibule," she said. "I'll join you there in a minute."

Waiting until she heard the vestibule door close with a metallic click, Jessie took a light, gauzy robe from her valise and slid from the bunk. She draped the robe over her shoulders and went to the end of the car, out the door. Coulter was waiting for her. Like Jessie, he'd put on a robe before leaving his bunk, and had slid his feet into a pair of bedroom slippers.

"I guess you think I've got a lot of brass," he said. "But I couldn't go to sleep for thinking about you, so close by and still so far away. I knew if I didn't take this chance, it's not likely I'd have another one. You're not mad, are you?"

"No woman who's honest enough to admit it ever gets really angry with a man she finds attractive," Jessie assured him. "It was just that—well, I wasn't expecting you to invite me."

"I lay there in my bunk thinking about you for a long time before I did," Coulter admitted. "Then, after I'd made up my mind that the worst you could do was say no, I got up enough spunk to ask you."

"I haven't said no yet," Jessie pointed out. "Do you think that by now you've gotten up enough spunk to kiss me?"

"Well, you just better guess I have!" Coulter replied. He demonstrated by grasping Jessie in his arms and pulling her to him, then bent forward and found her lips with his.

Already keyed up by the exciting events of the early part of the evening, Jessie did what her instinct told her to do. She responded at once to the kiss, thrusting out her tongue in search of Coulter's. After their lips had been pressed together for several moments, Jessie let her hand wander slowly down Coulter's side and slid it between their bodies to his crotch. The swelling she felt was more than satisfactory and after she'd fingered for a few minutes through the fabric of Coulter's robe, Jessie felt herself growing tense with anticipation after such a long period of abstinence.

"We're wasting our time staying out here," she whispered. "Shouldn't we go to my berth where we can be more comfortable?"

"We can't go too soon to suit me," Coulter replied. "I've been wanting to be with you ever since I got on this train."

Sliding into her berth, waiting for Coulter to shed his robe and join her, Jessie felt herself growing moist with anticipation. She slipped out of her robe and nightgown and lay down naked, waiting for him. In a moment the green curtains of the bunk swayed and Coulter slipped through them. His eyes widened when he saw Jessie lying nude in the dim light.

Before he had time to comment, Jessie grasped the hem of his nightshirt and pulled it above his waist. Sight of the jutting cylinder her move revealed was all the incentive she needed. Spreading her thighs, Jessie pulled Coulter down onto the bunk with her, and as he lurched forward she clasped her legs around his hips.

Positioning him quickly, Jessie tightened her leg muscles with a single quick jerk and drew him into her. Coulter's gasp of surprise at her unexpected assumption of the initiative in their lovemaking matched Jessie's long, deep sigh of satisfaction as he sank down on her warm, waiting body.

"Now drive!" she exhorted him in a whisper. "Drive and don't stop driving until daylight!"

Jessie's sighs grew deeper as Coulter obeyed. She brought her hips up, writhing, to meet his downward thrusts, gasping as she built quickly to the climax which seized her much sooner than she'd wanted it to. Again Coulter surprised her by being a more experienced lover than she'd anticipated. He slowed his tempo as she cried out in ecstasy and her body trembled to the peak of sensa-

33

tion, then held himself buried in her while her body grew quiet.

He did not start to stroke again until he'd roused her with soft caresses of his hands on her full budded breasts, and as Jessie quivered in response he began trailing kisses from the hollows at each side of her neck up to her cheeks and down her face to her lips. He continued his kisses until Jessie was once more fully aroused, her body trembling in anticipation, his swollen shaft still filling her.

Coulter moved more slowly this time, sinking into Jessie with long, deliberate penetrations, and her response was not as quick as it had been before. They found a rhythm that suited both of them, and rocked together slowly, wordlessly, until Jessie felt her partner beginning to quiver and sensed that he was rising to a climax.

She drew upon her geisha training again and tightened her inner muscles to increase their pleasure. When Coulter felt her gripping him he gasped and began driving faster, until Jessie's urgency matched his and they shuddered into a mutual climax.

Neither felt the need for words as they lay side by side, exhausted and pleasantly relaxed. Jessie was beginning to feel sleepy now. She turned to Coulter and asked, "Do you want to stay with me the rest of the night, or—"

Before she could finish her question, gaslight from the Pullman car's ceiling fixture flooded the berth as the green curtains were pulled aside and an unshaven, roughly dressed man appeared. Before either Jessie or Coulter could move, the newcomer whipped his revolver from its holster and covered them. He stared at them, a grin spreading over his grimy face.

"Damned if I ain't caught me a pair of lovebirds!" he said. "And the way things look right now, that's about all we're likely to get outa this job, so I guess you two better get on your duds and come along with me. Get a move on, you two! I ain't got all night to waste on you!"

"Who are you?" Jessie asked.

"I'm the one that's holding the gun, so I get to ask all the questions," the newcomer retorted. "Now roll outa there and get into your duds! You're about to take a little ride."

★

Chapter 4

"A ride to where?" Jessie asked as she groped for her clothing in the hammocklike net bag that hung along the back of the Pullman berth.

"You'll find out soon enough," their captor retorted. "Now get up and dress before you get me riled up at you!"

"My clothes are in the berth ahead," Coulter said. "Is it all right if I get them?"

"Go ahead and get into 'em." The man nodded. "But don't waste no time."

Jessie was already slipping her clothes on. She recognized the kind of gun-wielding outlaw they were facing, and had no doubt that he'd shoot if either she or Coulter tried to stall.

"We'd better do what he says," she told Coulter. "Not that we have any other choice."

Coulter was already on his feet in the aisle. He stepped across to his berth and started dressing. The outlaw who'd captured them divided his attention between the pair, his eyes shifting quickly from one to the other.

As soon as she'd realized that nothing could prevent the train robber from capturing them, Jessie had started racking her brain for a way to leave a message for Ki. Now, she took the only expedient that came to mind. After she'd slipped on her pantalettes and skirt, leaving her blouse lying over the holstered Colt and hiding it, she got out of the bunk.

Standing in the aisle, she faced their captor for a moment, distracting him by giving him a glimpse of her full breasts before she turned and bent down to pick up her blouse. While her body shielded the Colt from the outlaw's eyes, Jessie slid it under the pillow. The move took only a split second, then she turned quickly to face the captor again while she slipped her arms into the blouse and buttoned it.

"I'll give you this, lady," the bandit said as Jessie slid into the blouse. "You don't mind showing off what you got, and you sure have got a lot to show! Me and you are gonna get a lot better acquainted after we get to where we're going."

"And where might that be?" Jessie asked coolly.

"You'll find out soon enough," the man replied. "Now you just stand quiet while I take a look at your friend to see that he don't try no tricks either."

Coulter had put his trousers on hurriedly and had stuck his pistol in the waistband of the pants when the outlaw turned away from Jessie.

Raising the muzzle of his own pistol, the bandit snapped, "Hand over the gun, mister! You ain't going to need it where we're heading for."

A bit sheepishly, Coulter passed his pistol to the outlaw, who tucked it in the waistband of his own pants.

"Now get your feet into your shoes!" the man commanded. "I wasted enough time on you two as it is! Turn around and march to the back of the car. I'll be right behind you to see that you don't try no more smart tricks!"

Seeing no other alternative with the muzzle of the outlaw's revolver swinging to cover both her and Coulter, Jessie walked slowly down the aisle to the rear of the Pullman, trying to puzzle out the reason why the bandits had troubled to capture her and Coulter, and she got the answer when she went out onto the vestibule and saw a man on horseback waiting on the roadbed, holding the reins of three more horses.

"It's taken you long enough!" the mounted outlaw snapped. "I was just about ready to come after you!"

"I couldn't do it no faster," the man behind Jessie said. "Had to wait while these two put their togs on."

"You figure they're the best ones to grab?"

"They was the only ones that could pay the extra fare for the sleeping car, so I guess they can scrape up ransom money," their captor answered. "And you and me sure can't get into that baggage coach by ourselves. Now, let's quit palavering and get moving! This damn train's already due in Tehachapi, and when it don't pull in, the railroad's going to be sending somebody from there to see what's happened to it."

"Get 'em in the saddle, then, and we'll move off," the outlaw on the horse said. "By the time that train gets here from Tehachapi we'll be safe in the hideout, and there damn sure ain't nobody going to take 'em away from there."

"All right," the other replied. He prodded Jessie and Coulter with his revolver muzzle and went on, "One of you get on the paint and the other one take the roan. The dapple horse is mine."

Having no alternative, Jessie and Coulter mounted the horses and the bandit swung into his own saddle. The one who was apparently the leader turned to the captives.

"Likely you've figured out what's next," he said. "I'm going to lead and Ripsaw's going to follow, and you two'll be in between us. We got a ways to go and no time to waste, so if you figure to stay alive, you won't try no stunts. Now, move!"

For the next two hours, while the full moon climbed the sky and made the night almost daylight-bright, the horses carrying the outlaws and their captives pushed through the Tehachapi foothills. They traveled through some of the wildest, thickest brushland that Jessie had ever encountered. If the leader was following a trail, she was unable to see it, but the outlaw on the lead horse did not stop or even slow down a great deal. No matter how dense the scrub growth was, the man in front moved along unhesitatingly.

Dawn was beginning to brighten the small portion of the jagged horizon that Jessie could see through the dense underbrush when the man in front reined sharply aside and started down a narrow trail that seemed to start from nothing and lead nowhere. The ridge the trail followed was sinuous and sloped sharply. The little shelf was rocky, lined with loose stones. In places it was at most six feet wide, and at times it narrowed to less than half that, so they made slow progress.

By the time they reached the floor of the narrow, step-sided canyon into which they descended, the sky had brightened and the blush of sunrise was on the eastern sky. Suddenly the valley floor widened and ahead of them Jessie saw a huddle of weatherbeaten buildings: a house, an outhouse, a barn, and two sheds.

Leading the way to the barn, the leader rode through the open doors and swung out of his saddle.

"All right, you two can get down now," he announced. "I guess by now you seen there ain't no way you're going to get outa here by yourselves. Just don't try nothing smart, and you'll be all right. After we have breakfast, we'll set down and figure out how much ransom your folks will pay to get you back."

"What if there isn't anyone we can get to pay a ransom for us?" Jessie asked as they walked slowly toward the house.

"We ain't found nobody yet who don't have somebody outside that'll pay to get 'em free," the outlaw replied. "Or maybe whoever we've got has squirreled away some money they can come up with to buy their own way outa here."

"You've done this before, then?" Coulter asked.

"Now and again. When the haul from a job's short, like this one was."

"How long does it take to get a ransom arranged?" Jes-

40

sie wanted to know. "This place is so far away from everywhere that it must take quite as while."

"Oh, sometimes a month, maybe two," the man Jessie had heard called Ripsaw answered. "You're gonna be here long enough so's me and you can get a lot better acquainted."

"I won't say I'm looking forward to that," Jessie told him calmly.

"You'll get used to it after we've cozied up a few times," the outlaw promised with a wide grin. "Just wait and see."

"If you don't like old Ripsaw here, maybe you'll cotton up to me," his companion put in, grinning at Jessie. His lips were parted wide enough to give her a glimpse of two gaps in his crooked front teeth. "Or Cottle. He's inside, so you ain't got a look at him yet."

"Now just hush that flap-mouth of yours, Verdis," Ripsaw snapped. "I seen her first and grabbed her! That ain't all, I seen her bare-ass naked, and what I seen, I don't aim to share with you and Cottle nor nobody else!"

"You know damned well that ain't the way we do things here, Ripsaw!" Verdis replied. "As long as we keep her, we'll pass her around, share and share alike!"

"Well, maybe I'll dig into what I got stashed away and buy your shares off both of you, then," Ripsaw said.

"And maybe we won't sell!" Verdis retorted. "I ain't so sure I would, and there might be others feels the same way."

"That'll be for Mason and the other boys to say after they get back from that bank job," Ripsaw told his companion. "And I reckon Mason's gonna be the only boss we'll have, now that Henry got his tonight."

"We'll just have to wait and see about that, won't we?" Verdis commented.

"Hold on, you two!" Coulter broke in. "You men can't buy and sell this young lady like she was nothing but a—a piece of merchandise!"

41

"I reckon you're going to stop us?" Verdis asked, his voice edged with anger.

Coulter opened his mouth to reply, but could think of nothing to say, and closed it sheepishly. Jessie had said nothing during the argument between the two train robbers. She'd been in similar situations before, and had learned that the least attention she drew to herself, the better.

By this time they'd reached the door of the farmhouse. It swung open and a man stepped out onto the porch. Like the other two, he had on a butternut-cloth shirt and the blue jeans that Levi Strauss had made popular among miners and other Western workers. He was a broad man, rounded at all edges, but had a beefiness that hinted at stout muscles below his layer of fat. His face was swathed in bandages that slanted across part of his head and covered one eye and ear, but the eye that was visible was colder than blue ice.

"Where's the rest of 'em?" he asked Verdis and Ripsaw after he'd given Jessie and Coulter a quick glance.

"They got it, Cottle," Ripsaw said curtly. "We lost Burgin and his hoss before we got the damn train stopped. Henry and Sanchez was killed in the baggage car."

"How in the hell could a plain job go so sour?" the man called Cottle asked. When both Ripsaw and Verdis shook their heads and shrugged, he went on angrily, "I told Henry he was cutting it too fine, with me not fit to go along! Damn it, he ought to've waited till Mason got back from that bank job!"

"Well, we done all right at first," Ripsaw said. "Stopped the train like we figured to, but then Burgin got killed, and before me and Verdis could shake down the passengers, the damn conductor and some Chink that was on board bushwhacked Henry and Sanchez while they was trying to open the safe. Soon as we found out they was dead, we grabbed these two and hurried on back."

"These was the only ones that was in the sleeping car," Verdis added. "And anyhow, we only had two spare

42

horses. We couldn't've brought back any more."

"So we'll take what we get, the same as we do when any job goes sour," Ripsaw went on. "Now, let's give these two a bite of something to eat, mainly to keep 'em quiet. If Verdis feels like I do, we're going to catch up on the sleep we lost."

Inside the little windowless shanty where Jessie and Coulter were sitting, the light was so dim they could barely see one another across the few feet that separated them. Their legs were stretched out in front of them on the dirt floor, their ankles bound with rope. Even sitting up was uncomfortable with their wrists lashed behind their backs, but in spite of the discomfort of their positions they'd both slept in utter exhaustion for the first few hours following their confinement.

Now, with the late afternoon sunlight beginning to spread across the floor from the wide crack under the door, enough brightness trickled in to allow them to make out each others' features.

"Those outlaws have certainly left us alone a long time," Coulter said when he saw that Jessie was awake.

"I imagine they needed sleep even worse than we did," she replied. "They had to make the trip between here and the railroad both ways. We only made it once."

"That's something I hadn't thought of." He nodded. "But maybe they'll stay away a while longer. I could still use a bit more rest, and I'll bet you could, too."

"It'd be nice, but not really necessary," Jessie said. "I think we'd be better off trying to figure out a way to get out of here instead of sleeping."

"I've been trying to think of a way to answer them when they begin asking us who's going to pay a ransom to get us out of here," Coulter told her. "The sad fact of the matter is that nobody, except maybe my employer, is interested enough in me to pay them a lot of money to turn me loose."

43

"Don't worry about that," Jessie said. "I'll pay your ransom as well as mine, if you'll just keep quiet about knowing my name."

"I don't understand," Coulter said, his brow knitted. "Why would you do a thing like that?"

"My name happens to be fairly well known," she explained. "I remember mentioning it when we introduced ourselves on the train, but I hope you've forgotten it by now."

"I haven't, of course," Coulter replied. Then, his frown deepening as he stared at Jessie, he said, "But don't worry. I won't tell them what it is."

"Please don't think I'm being mean or unfeeling when I ask you if you're sure you can keep from talking even if they make all sorts of threats. Or, for that matter, even if they carry out their threats. Are you really sure you can keep quiet?"

"If it's important to you, I can sure try," Coulter said soberly. "Even if I still don't quite understand."

"You will, after we escape and get back to civilization," Jessie promised. "But right now, please just take my word that it's important."

"Sure I will, if it's that important to you. But you seem to be real sure we're going to escape." Coulter frowned. "I don't see how you can be so positive."

"As soon as Ki realizes we've been captured, he'll start looking for us. It may take him a while to find us, but he won't give up. If we can just hold out until he gets here, we'll be all right."

"This is all just guesswork," Coulter said. "How do you know your man Ki is going to find us?"

"Because I know Ki," Jessie replied calmly.

This time Coulter did not reply, but simply stared and shook his head. "I guess you know what you're talking about," he said. "But I sure don't see how one man's going to be much help to us."

"You'll understand later," Jessie assured him. "But

while we're waiting, we might as well be trying to work out a plan."

"What kind of plan?"

"Things we can do to try to get away without waiting for Ki. I'm sure we're smarter than these outlaws," Jessie said.

"Do you have some ideas?" Coulter asked.

"Of course. One of them is to see if we can get rid of these ropes we're tied up with. Suppose you start working your way over here toward me, and I'll move toward you."

For a moment Coulter watched Jessie as she leaned forward and pulled herself a few inches away from the wall by holding her heels firmly against the floor and bending her knees to pull herself forward. The third or fourth time Jessie moved, Coulter got the idea and copied her motions. Small as the shack was, it took several long minutes of agonizing, inch-by-inch progress before their bound feet met near the center of the little shack. They stopped when their feet touched and slouched forward to rest their aching leg muscles.

"Well, we're close together now," Coulter told Jessie. His voice was less uncertain than before. "What do we do next?"

"You sit still. I'll wriggle around behind you, where I can get to the rope around your wrists."

When Jessie tried to move, she found that making progress sideways was much more difficult than simply inching ahead. Not until she lay down and rolled, kicking with her feet as best she could, did she manage to get around Coulter's bound figure and inch up to him until they sat back-to-back.

"Can you feel the knots in the rope on my wrists?" she asked. "I can't quite reach yours."

"I don't know. Let me try."

Jessie felt Coulter's fingers moving over her hands until he'd located the rope that was wrapped around her wrists.

"I think I've got my fingers on the knots," he said after

45

a few more moments of exploring. "Let me rest my fingers for a few minutes before I try untying them."

After what seemed an agonizingly long period of fumbling, Jessie felt the tugging of Coulter's fingertips on the rope that imprisoned her wrists, and several minutes later the coils that immobilized her arms grew slack. Flexing her forearms as best she could, she felt the rope go slack at last, and with a few quick twists freed her wrists from their bonds.

"We've done it!" she exclaimed. "Let me get my ankles untied, then I'll free you."

By now the lines of mottled, reflected sunlight that crept in through the wide crack below the door had brightened the little shack's interior enough to let Jessie see what she was doing. In spite of the stiffness of her cramped fingers, she made quick work of untying Coulter's wrists. In another few minutes she was helping him to untie the ropes around his ankles. He scrambled to his feet and stood unsteadily, swaying a bit, while his legs trembled. Then, as the cramps in his calves and thighs faded and feeling returned to his feet, he straightened up.

"I guess I'm about as good as ever," he told Jessie. "But what're we going to do next? Those outlaws in the house have guns. We don't have anything but our bare hands."

"Yes, I know." Jessie nodded. She was moving to the door as she spoke. It had no knob, only a small chunk of wood that served as a handle. She pulled at the wood chunk, then pushed the door, but it did not yield. Turning back to Coulter, she went on, "It's barred on the outside. I guess I knew it would be, but I had to try it. We don't have much time, you know. It's not going to be very long before one of them comes out here to check up on us."

"Let me give it a try," he said, stepping up to the door beside her. "Maybe I can break it open."

"That bar on the outside's not going to give easily, and it'll make a lot of noise if we try to break it."

"If only we had some kind of weapon!" Coulter said.

46

He gestured with a sweeping movement of his hand that took in the barren interior of the little shed. "A gun or knife—even a club would be better than nothing!"

When Coulter waved his hand, Jessie's eyes followed its sweeping gesture in the natural reflex triggered by such movements. As her eyes swept the hut, she got a fugitive glimpse of something in one of its corners. She stepped over to the corner to investigate.

"We're not entirely weaponless," she said. Reaching into the gloomy corner, she took out a twig broom and held it out.

"A broom?" Coulter frowned as he looked at it. The broom was homemade, a bundle of thin, flexible twigs bound around one end of the straight section of an inch-round branch cut from a tree. Shaking his head, he went on, "It's too thin to make a decent club. As far as I can see, it's not good for anything but sweeping."

Jessie's fingers were already working at the twisted end of the wire that circled the ends of the twigs and bound them to the branch. She began flexing the tightly crimped pigtail of wire that squeezed the top of the bundle tightly and held it to the end of the five-foot long branch. The wire snapped at last, and she shook the branch to dislodge the twigs. As they dropped to the dirt floor, Jessie held the branch out for Coulter to see.

"That's good, stiff wood," she said. "It'll make a first-class *bo*. I'm not as good with it as Ki is, but I can use it fairly well. We'll give those outlaws the kind of greeting they don't expect!"

★

Chapter 5

"I know a broom handle when I see one, but I never heard of a *bo*," Coulter said, frowning.

"It's an Oriental weapon, something like a broomstick, but much, much better."

"And you think that stick of wood will pass for one?"

"I'm sure it will."

Shaking his head, Coulter said, "I don't see how it can be of much use to us."

"You'd be surprised what a *bo* can do when an expert uses it," Jessie said. "I still have a lot to learn, but Ki's taught me a bit about it."

"I guess you know what you're talking about," Coulter told her, shaking his head. "But I still don't see that stick being much good to us."

Before Jessie could reply, the sound of a slamming door came from the direction of the house, and footsteps thudded on the ground outside, growing steadily louder.

"We may be glad we have it before too long," Jessie said calmly. "I have a hunch the outlaws have finally gotten around to coming after us. But from the sound of those footsteps, my guess is there's only one of them."

"Stand back from the door, then!" Coulter said. "I'll do the best I can to take care of him!"

"No!" Jessie exclaimed, keeping her voice down. "Just let him swing it open, and I'll get him with the *bo!*"

By now the footsteps were just outside the door. They stopped, and the grating squeak of the bar being raised reached their ears. Then the door swung open, and Ripsaw started into the shack. He got a glimpse of Jessie and Coulter standing inside the hut, and his mouth opened. Whatever he'd intended to say was never uttered, because Jessie was ready for him.

Holding the improvised *bo* horizontal just above waist level, she jabbed its end into the outlaw's stomach with all her considerable strength. Ripsaw's exclamation was smothered in the grunt of pain that burst from his throat, and he bent double with the pain of the *bo*'s jab into his diaphragm. Sweeping his arms wide, he grabbed at the sides of the doorway to keep himself from falling.

This was the reaction Jessie had expected. The instant her first blow went home she'd yanked the *bo* back, and when the outlaw bent forward, his hands clutching his midsection, she twirled the *bo* in a half-circle and slammed Ripsaw with a blow on the back of his head. The noise of the wood meeting his skull sounded almost as loud as a pistol shot.

For a moment the outlaw's big hands held their grip on the doorframe. Jessie had not let the whirling *bo* lose the momentum of its swing. Reversing her hands with a twinkle of movement, she kept her grip on the *bo*'s center and brought the opposite end around and up to smash into Ripsaw's face while he was still immobile and bending double with his head exposed.

Blood spurted from Ripsaw's nose as the tip of the *bo* shattered its fragile bones. Dancing in a half-step to one side of the toppling man, the *bo* still moving in the arc that would complete its circle, Jessie landed her third blow at the base of Ripsaw's skull, and the outlaw collapsed like a poleaxed ox.

"Let's go!" Jessie said to Coulter, who was still standing frozen in amazement in the center of the shack. "If we run for the barn, maybe we can get horses and be away from here before the others miss us!"

Without waiting to see whether Coulter was following, Jessie stepped over Ripsaw's recumbent form and started toward the barn. After she'd gone a few running steps, she looked back to make sure that Coulter was following her. He was, but as Jessie swiveled her head she saw something else. Cottle was standing in the doorway of the house, watching the shed. He'd seen Jessie, and his hand was moving to his holstered pistol.

There was nothing that Jessie could do to stop the outlaw from drawing. She bent down and kept running, glancing back to see where Coulter was. He'd seen Cottle, too, and had changed his course to veer toward the house.

When Jessie looked in the direction Coulter was taking and saw Cottle again, the outlaw had his revolver in his hand and was swinging it toward Coulter. Jessie veered off her course and started for the house.

Then, before Cottle could level the heavy revolver, she saw a streak of bright steel flashing through the air, catching the red rays of the dropping sun. Before she could release the sigh of relief that formed in her throat, the streaking steel disk of the *shuriken* had reached its mark. It sliced into Cottle's throat, bringing a bright spurt of arterial blood.

Cottle's gunhand sagged and his finger tightened on the trigger of his pistol as he fell forward. The revolver roared, its barrel spurted flame, and the slug kicked up a spurt of dirt only inches from Coulter's feet.

As Cottle fell sprawling, his pistol falling to the ground from nerveless fingers, Verdis burst through the door. He was bringing up his revolver as he emerged from the opening, his head swiveling as he looked for a target, but a second flash of bright steel was already on its way. The razor-edged *shuriken* caught Verdis in the outer corner of one eye. One tip of the star-shaped blade sliced into the

51

corner of his eye socket, and when momentum kept the blade turning the next tip was deflected into the fragile bones of his temple. It sank in, cutting through them and stabbing into the outlaw's brainpan.

Verdis staggered, his arms dropping limply to his sides, and he collapsed and fell on top of Cottle's body.

Jessie stopped now and looked at Coulter. He'd halted, too, and was staring in slack-jawed astonishment at the bodies on the steps of the farmhouse.

Turning her head toward the barn, Jessie called loudly, "I'm glad you got here in time, Ki. For a while, I didn't think you'd make it."

"For a while I didn't think I would myself," Ki replied, coming out of the shed that was a twin to the one in which Jessie and Coulter had been confined and starting toward them. "It wasn't what you'd call an easy trip. It was lucky that the outlaws left one of their horses behind, so I didn't have to make it on foot, and that the horse knew the trail here better than I did."

"This place is the headquarters of that Mason-Henry gang the conductor was telling us about, all right," Jessie said as Ki stopped beside her and Coulter. "The outlaws were talking like we weren't there to hear what they said, and we found out that one of the men killed in the baggage car was Henry, and that the other leader, Mason, is off somewhere with the rest of the gang pulling another robbery."

"Then unless you want to stay here and wait for the rest of them, we'd better start moving," Ki said.

Jessie shook her head. "It's more important for us to get on to San Francisco, Ki. But perhaps when we get back to the train, Mr. Coulter will stay and guide a posse to this place."

"I sure will!" Coulter said quickly. "As a matter of fact, Jessie, what happened to that train last night has sort of changed my ideas a little bit. I want to stop being a furniture drummer and go to work as a lawman."

"I think you'd make a good one, Avery." She nodded. "And gangs like this one certainly do have to be stopped."

"That's my idea exactly!" Coulter told her. "And I guess helping finish off the Mason-Henry gang is as good as way as any to start."

"It is," Jessie agreed. She turned back to Ki and asked, "I guess your horse is somewhere close by?"

"Tethered a little way from here, by the trail."

"Then we'll saddle two more for Avery and me. We ought to be able to make it back to the railroad in time to get on a train for San Francisco tonight. I'm anxious now to get to San Francisco and spend a day or two just resting before we start for the High Sierras."

"I'm sorry it took us so long to get to San Francisco, Frank," Jessie told her attorney after they'd exchanged greetings and she'd settled into a chair beside Allison's massive, highly polished desk. "But now I'm ready to listen while you explain exactly what kind of problem you've dug up for me this time."

"I wouldn't say that 'dug up' is the best phrase to describe this one, Jessie." Allison smiled as he reached into his desk drawer and brought out a manila file folder. "Nobody with eyes could miss seeing that advertisement I sent you, so I didn't have to do any digging to find it. And from what you said in your telegram, you were as upset as I was when I saw it for the first time."

"Has the ad been repeated since then?" Jessie asked.

"Oh, yes. Several times."

"And isn't there anything you can do to stop it?"

Allison shook his head. "I'm afraid not. You see, the promoter who's using your father's name actually has an option giving him the right to buy the land he claims the gold deposits are on. It's authentic, too. I've seen it myself, and I know Alex's signature almost as well as I do my own."

"You mean that Alex simply signed an option without

53

limiting its life?" Jessie frowned. "That's not like him. He was always very careful in his business dealings."

"Oh, I agree with you," Allison said, nodding. "But apparently he had something else on his mind when he signed this one. And if you remember, I wasn't representing Alex when the option was signed. Old Judge Carrol was, and he was far past his best years when this particular option was executed."

"I certainly don't want the Starbuck name attached to some kind of swindler's scheme," Jessie said soberly. "And that's what this one appears to be."

"I'm sure it is." The lawyer nodded. "If there were any workable gold deposits on that land around Sierra City, Alex would have known about them and held on to the land."

"Now just a minute!" Jessie protested. "First of all, I'm not quite sure what you mean when you say 'workable deposits.'"

"Gold's not a bit of good to anybody unless it's mined, Jessie," the lawyer replied. "There are some reasons I'll get to in a minute that will explain the situation better."

"All right, I'm not impatient. But I thought the land itself was still mine." Jessie frowned. "That's the impression I got from your letter."

"It is," Allison agreed. "The option simply covers the mineral rights. It's equivalent to a land lease, and the promoter of this gold-mining scheme pays an annual lease fee. The fee is very low, by the way, only a few hundred dollars a year, but as long as it's paid the option on the mineral rights can't be rescinded."

"You know, Frank. I simply can't understand how all this business of land sales and mineral rights came about," Jessie said. "It somehow doesn't seem like the kind of thing Alex would get into. Perhaps you'd better give me the history of it."

"That's very easy to do," Allison said. "Especially since I just had my head clerk dig into old Judge Carrol's files—

54

we acquired them from his estate when we took over his law practice after he died, of course."

"Go ahead, then," Jessie said.

"You were still going to school in the East when this happened," the attorney began. "So it's no wonder you're not familiar with what went on then. Alex was very, very busy at that time, and he needed a place where he could be isolated from all the business pressures he was under."

"But that's why he bought the ranch," Jessie said when Allison paused. "The Circle Star."

"This was before he found the Circle Star," Allison went on. "Alex's business headquarters were still in San Francisco then. He wanted a place close by where he could go for a few days and just rest. And Sierra City seemed to be ideal, because it was only a few hours by train from the city."

"So I understand." Jessie nodded. "But I'd never heard of Sierra City until I got that newspaper ad you sent me."

"No wonder. Sierra City died officially back in the 1860s, when the town was deserted."

"Deserted? Why? Didn't they find any gold close by?"

"Oh, there was plenty of gold." Allison smiled. "But not what prospectors and miners call 'workable' gold."

"I always thought gold was just gold all over the world," Jessie commented. "Exactly what is 'workable' gold, Frank?"

"Gold dust that's panned from stream bottoms is very workable because it's almost always pure gold," Allison told her. "Gold ore from mines—well, it's like the copper ore you get from your mines in New Mexico, Jessie. It has to go to a smelter where rocks and dirt and other impurities are separated from the gold."

"That I can understand." Jessie nodded. "But smelting is a very common branch of mining. I don't see how that would have any effect on gold mining around Sierra City."

"There were two things wrong up there," Allison explained. "The gold ore was in quartz formations, so it

55

couldn't be panned. The other thing was the weather. It starts snowing up at Sierra City in September or October, and by December the town is usually buried under drifts that stand twenty to thirty feet deep. The snow at that altitude—about nine thousand feet, I understand—doesn't melt until June or July. There's no quartz-separation mill ever made that can operate profitably if it can be run only three months out of the year, and snowdrifts twenty feet deep aren't overcome that easily."

"But the gold really was there?"

"Oh, yes," Allison said. "It still is there, and it'll stay right where it is until somebody can work out a way to get it separated from the quartz."

"But you just said that the gold was discovered twenty or thirty years ago," Jessie objected. "Surely more modern and more efficient ways to mill it have been worked out since then!"

Allison shook his head. "Oh, there have been a lot of improvements in smelting, of course, but none that will get out enough gold in three months of the year to make it profitable to build a smelter in such an isolated place."

"We've gotten away from Sierra City, though," Jessie said thoughtfully. "What happened to it?"

"I'm sure it's still there," the attorney replied. "My clerk ran across an old clipping while he was going over Judge Carrol's files. It told about a man named Snowshoe Thompson who used to carry the mail over the Sierras in the winter, before the railroad was built. He saw Sierra City in midwinter, soon after all the people left."

"And what did he find?"

"He found the place had been abandoned in such a hurry that all the people just walked away—on snowshoes, I suppose—and left their houses furnished: beds, chairs, divans and tables, even curtains and chinaware and all the rest of their belongings. They must've really been anxious to get away."

56

"That sounds like something out of a fairy tale!" Jessie objected. "I just can't believe it."

"I've been told the town's still standing, though," Allison went on. "I wrote to my correspondent attorneys in the neighborhood, in Truckee and Virginia City, and they say that Sierra City is still there."

"And it still belongs to me, I suppose?"

"Of course it does," the lawyer assured her. "I've had the records checked very thoroughly. It stands right in the middle of almost thirty thousand acres of land that Alex bought all those years ago. Apparently he simply lost interest in the Sierras after he decided he preferred the Circle Star."

"Yes, Alex fell in love with the ranch the first time he saw it. He must've just brushed everything else aside to attend to later, since he was so anxious to get things finished at the Circle Star so he could move there, and after he did he always considered the ranch his home."

"Well, it looks like the next move is up to you, Jessie," Allison said after he'd riffled through the sheaf of papers in his folder. "I can understand why you don't want the Starbuck name used in connection with this gold-mining promotion, which is a swindle on the face of it."

"That's one of the things I want to ask you about," Jessie said. "After all these years, how can this promoter's deal with Alex still stand up?"

"California law is peculiar in one respect," the lawyer told her. "Back in the gold-rush days, when all the forty-niners were staking claims like wildfire, the legislature was trying to protect everybody concerned. They passed a law back then that as long as a gold claim was properly staked, whoever owned the land was to be paid a share of any gold taken from a claim on their property. They included a clause in the law giving miners the right to prospect and work any claims they staked, even on private land. Then in another paragraph they included a stipulation that the landowner could sell the property as long as the buyer agreed to honor the miner's rights to keep working his claim regardless of land transfers."

"Something for everybody, you might say," Jessie commented.

"Exactly," Allison said. "What it comes down to is that you own the land and will get a share of any gold discovered on it, but as long as there's a valid gold-rights claim, you're forced to honor it."

"In other words, I've got to honor this man's right to keep prospecting, but if gold is ever produced, I'll get a share."

"That's about what it amounts to. His name is Clem Harney, by the way. You can try to buy back the option Alex gave him, but my hunch is that he's the kind who'd really hold you up if he thought he had you in a bind."

"Which is exactly what I am in, it seems," Jessie said thoughtfully. "No matter what I do, it seems that this Clem Harney is in control of the situation."

"From your standpoint, he is, as long as he holds that option Alex gave him."

"I'm paying you for legal advice, Frank, so suppose you give me some," Jessie said after a moment of studying her situation.

"My advice is this: Either forget about the ads Harney's running, or go up to Sierra City and try to buy back the option he has," Allison replied.

"If I try to buy the option, he'll know he has me at his mercy and will try to get a big price for it." Jessie frowned.

"I'm sure he will," the attorney agreed. "The question you're going to have to answer is, do you want to pay his price? If you think it's too high, we can try to tie his operation up with an injunction, which would put you in a better bargaining position."

"But from the way you've explained the situation, I'd still lose in the end, wouldn't I?"

"I'm afraid you would. The law regarding mining

claims is very clear, and it's been tested in court in quite a number of cases. The only legal way you can get this Clem Harney to surrender his option is to buy it back from him. And since he seems to have a good thing going, I'm sure he wouldn't sell."

"Oh, I'm as sure of that as you are," Jessie agreed. "In fact, I'm not even sure yet that I want to offer to buy it. All I really want to do is stop him from using Alex's name in his advertising."

"I don't know of any way you can do that without taking him to court," Allison said. "And that would just create more publicity for his scheme."

"Then I won't waste anything but a little time by going up and taking a look at the situation before I make up my mind," Jessie said decisively. "And that's what I'll do. Ki and I will be on the train to the Sierras in the morning."

★

Chapter 6

"We ought to be getting very close to Sierra City by now, Ki," Jessie said as their horses struggled along the steep grade of the narrow dirt trail that wound in a zigzag up the slope.

"From what the fellow at the livery stable in Truckee told us, we should be there about dark," Ki replied. "And the day's just about over now."

They reached the top of the grade and reined in to let the horses breathe. Ahead there were still more mountains, their ragged crests silhouetted against the cloudless blue sky. From the point where they'd stopped, the ground fell away sharply, the trail they'd been following showing below them as a narrow, zigzagging streak of brown on the steep slope they'd just finished mounting.

Following the directions of the liveryman at Truckee, where they'd rented the horses they were riding, Jessie and Ki had been able to follow the well-beaten road up the rugged flanks of the giant range with no trouble. The road itself was well marked by the rutted tracks of the ore wagons that had hauled silver ore from the Comstock Lode in its beginning days, before smelters had built on the Nevada side of the mountains.

After the road was cut over the high humps, the huge ore wagons with their six- and eight-mule hitches had left deep ruts in the thin layer of soil that covered the stone heart of the Sierra Nevadas, forming a road that followed the easiest grades to their peaks and descended to the smelters on the California side of the range. Late in the day, they'd left the well-beaten road to take the narrower but still well-defined track that would lead to their destination.

They'd seen the first signs pointing to Sierra City at a fork where the main road, with its deep-cut ruts left by the ore wagons, led around a ridge to disappear to the northwest and the smelters on the California side of the Sierras. A newer road, little more than a trace, turned sharply upward and wound back and forth in a series of zigzags to the crest of the ridge. From that point it leveled out to the next in the series of ridges that still rose above them.

"I can see why these mountains would have attracted Alex," Jessie remarked as they passed the second sign indicating that their goal was still ahead. "It's so quiet up here that a sneeze would sound like an explosion."

Below them the flanks of the seemingly endless mountains showed the tops of the giant trees that made up the pine forest. It was a waving sea of green, rippling gently in the light breeze of late afternoon. All that broke the verdant expanse was the erratic course of a little river that flowed down the sides of the rugged rising hills, a streak of blue interrupted here and there by patches of white froth, created by shallow spots where the stream was only a few inches deep and ran in a bed of stones.

To Jessie, accustomed to the vastness of the Southwest Texas prairie around the Circle Star, the mountains seemed to be secretive, hiding untold places in the creases of hundreds of valleys that cut the raw flanks stretching up to their serrated crests. The small whispering murmur of the late-afternoon breeze was broken now and then by the sharp thunking of a lumberman's axe somewhere below them. As Jessie and Ki sat letting their horses breathe, the sound of a crash reached their ears, the long-drawn-out noise of a falling tree.

Jessie tensed as the unexpected sounds broke the stillness of the pine forest, then she realized what she'd heard and turned to Ki to say, "I suppose that logging and prospecting are about all we'll find up here. That's probably what Alex liked about this part of the Sierras—they're almost as isolated as the Circle Star."

"Except that they're a lot harder to get to," Ki replied. "And to travel through. I don't mind telling you that I'll be glad when we finally get to Sierra City. It seems like we've been on this trail for a week instead of just an afternoon."

"We shouldn't have much farther to go," Jessie said. "At least we can see the peak lines of the ridges now."

"We'd better move on, then," Ki told her. "At the rate we're moving on these steep grades we'll be lucky to get to Sierra City before dark, and I'd hate to try to follow this road without being able to see where I'm going."

Toeing their horses ahead, they moved up the steadily steepening grade. In addition to the gleaming fresh paint on the newer signs that assured them that Sierra City still lay ahead, there were other, older signs, not painted on freshly cut boards, but left from the days before the area's promise of rich, gold-laden ore had proved to be an illusion. Long-deserted diggings showed clearly on the flanks of the steadily steepening ridges that flanked the trail.

After her visits to the Starbuck copper mines in New Mexico, the signs of mining were plain to Jessie. The only difference between these abandoned diggings and the mines in the more southerly state was the quantity of the tailings that streaked from them down the sides of the steep slopes.

In the active mines, the heaps of tailings were both wide and high. Here the piles of tailings were much smaller, and the elements had leveled them until they formed only small, streaked humps on the steeply slanting ground.

"You know, Ki, I'm just as glad that these gold deposits turned out to be unworkable," Jessie remarked as they passed the tailings that marked some disappointed prospector's abandoned claim. "This country is too beautiful to let it be spoiled by what I've seen in other places."

"From what Frank Allison told you, it's going to be this way for a long time," Ki replied. "Unless this Harney fellow we're looking for knows something that nobody else does."

"I doubt that's possible," Jessie said. "I think the forests on these mountainsides will stay undisturbed for a long time to come."

They were nearing the top of an unusually high ridge a few minutes later when the trail took a sudden twist that led along the base of the ridge to a break. They entered the narrow V, and had ridden for less than a quarter of a mile when it widened suddenly. Ahead they could see the green sward of a well-grassed meadow, and beyond it the glints of blue that marked the waters of a small lake. In the grassy sweep between the gap they'd passed through and the waters of the lake there stood a ragged line of weather-beaten buildings.

Jessie turned to Ki and said, "I think we're finally at the end of our trip. Unless I'm badly mistaken, we've just arrived at Sierra City."

Ki looked beyond Jessie at the houses. Most of them stood in roughly parallel rows on each side of the trail that cut across the shallow mountain meadow, but a few had been built in the meadow itself. With the exception of a two-story building that was near the end of the double row, the dwellings were small, compact single-story structures. All the houses seemed to be empty and there were no people in sight. Then Ki saw the glint of water beyond the dwellings and pointed it out to Jessie.

"Yes, I noticed the lake, too," she said. "But the place certainly looks deserted."

"As old Gimpy back at the Circle Star would say, 'It don't look like such a much to me,'" Ki agreed.

Most of the houses did indeed look like they were little

more than shacks. The shingles on almost all the roofs were curled up at the edges, and two or three had enough shingles missing to expose the rafters below. Even at a distance it was obvious that the lumber used in the construction of a majority of the dwellings had not been seasoned, for there were wide gaps between the siding boards.

All the houses, from best to worst, showed evidence that they'd been hastily constructed. None of them had been painted, and in several the windows yawned blankly, glassless. On some the wide pine boards that had been used as siding were warped and twisted. Fewer than half of them boasted brick chimneys, the others had sections of stovepipe extending from the walls, with other sections added vertically to carry the smoke above the eaves line.

"Considering what Frank Allison told me about the way this place was built practically overnight and abandoned almost at once, I'd say it's in pretty good shape, though," Jessie went on. "Even if it does look ghostly and deserted."

"My guess is that if anyone's around, they'll be in that big house down at the far end," Ki said. "Even if there's no smoke coming out of the chimney, it has the look of being occupied. Maybe we'd better go down there and see if I'm right."

Walking their horses, they moved on toward the biggest of the buildings. The sound of hoofbeats in the usually silent forest must have alerted the occupant of the house to their approach, for Jessie and Ki were still a good distance from the building when a man stepped out of the doorway and stood waiting for them. He was roughly dressed, wearing a wool shirt and a pair of Levi's miner's dungarees tucked into laced boots.

Under her breath, Jessie said, "In a way, I hope that's not the man we're looking for. I'd like to talk to some of the people who've answered his newspaper advertising before I spend too much time with him."

"You'll manage to find out what you want to know,

regardless of who it is," Ki told her confidently. "But get your story ready, because we're almost near enough now to start talking."

As though the man they were approaching had heard Ki's words, he called to them even before Jessie could reply to her companion. At close range Jessie could see that he was younger than he'd appeared to be at first. He was tall, bulky, and clean-shaven, though now in need of a shave. He wore no hat, and both his hair and the stubble on his face showed bronze in the sunlight. His jaw was firm, and his hair was beginning to recede. Jessie guessed him to be in his late thirties, for with the exception of squint lines at the corners of his blue eyes his deeply tanned face was almost unlined.

"Howdy, folks!" he said heartily. "It's nice to see some new faces up here. I hope you didn't have too much trouble finding the place."

"No trouble at all," Jessie replied. "Of course, the signs were a big help."

"I told Clem they'd be," the greeter replied. "He didn't want to go to the trouble, but he saw what I was talking about when I reminded him that a lot of the folks who come up here are city people who haven't had much experience on a mountain trail."

"You're not Clem Harney, then?" Jessie asked.

"Sorry, ma'am. Clem's down in Los Angeles or San Francisco right now, but I'm looking for him back any day. My name's Matt Bolton. I sorta keep an eye on things while Clem's gone."

Faced with the need for an instant decision on whether to give her name or stay anonymous for the moment, Jessie straddled the truth. She said, "My name is Jessie, Mr. Bolton, and this is Ki, who helps me with my business affairs. I came up here to find out about those gold-mining claims Mr. Harney's been advertising in the newspapers."

Bolton made no pretense of hiding his interest in what

to him must have seemed an oddly assorted pair. His eyes flicked from Jessie to Ki and back to Jessie for a moment before he spoke again. Then he nodded slowly.

"Pleased to make your acquaintance, Miz Jessie," he said. "You, too, Ki. But I don't answer good to mister. My men all call me Matt, and I guess maybe you oughta do the same."

"Your men?" Jessie frowned, looking around at the silent, deserted dwellings.

"My lumber-jacks ain't working around here," Bolton told her. "My logging stand's quite a ways down the slope, and the timber crews stay at the bunkhouse there because it's close to where we're cutting timber."

"I see." Jessie nodded. From her familiarity with the Starbuck logging operations in Oregon and Washington, she recognized the truth of Bolton's statements. It was a pattern quite common in timbering operations. Many of the Starbuck properties had several logging camps distant from a central supervisory office. "But you come up and look after things here when Mr. Harney has to be away?"

"That's about the way it is, ma'am. And Clem's not gone enough to put me out none. But I don't mix into his business any more'n he does in mine, so I'm afraid I can't help you much if you've come up here to talk about the gold claims."

"Perhaps we'd better go back to Truckee, Jessie," Ki suggested. "We can get rooms there in the hotel and wait for Harney to show up."

"Now, you don't have to go all the way back to Truckee," Bolton protested. "It's a good thirty miles, and you sure can't make it today."

"No, we've spent all afternoon on the road up here," Jessie said. "But what did you have in mind, Matt?"

Bolton indicated the straggling lines of houses on the meadow. "Pick out any one of them that suits your fancy and bunk down right here till Clem gets back," he said. "It won't cost you a penny. He don't charge rent to anybody who comes up here to look at his gold claims."

"You make it sound even better than it did a minute ago," Jessie said.

"Oh, there's no trick about it, Miss Jessie," Bolton told them. "I don't know how you're fixed for grub, but if you're short, Clem keeps some things on hand here that he sells to the people who come up, just a convenience, like. There's a room in this old hotel where he's living that was fixed up to keep ice in, but I don't think he's using it. Anyhow, I know he's got airtights and flour and cornmeal and rice and potatoes. If you need more'n there is in his stuff, it's a lot closer to my timber camp than it is to Truckee, and you'll find most anything you'd want in my commissary stock."

"All these houses are vacant, then?" Jessie asked, indicating the rows of dwellings.

"All but this one Clem uses. I use it too, when I come up here and stay over for a day or two. There's plenty of rooms in it, so we don't get in each other's way."

"Staying here would certainly be a better idea than going back to Truckee," Ki said to Jessie. "We have enough food for a day or two, and if we can get supplies as Mr. Bolton says, it'd solve our problem."

"If you make up your mind to stay, just move into any of the houses that strikes your fancy," Bolton repeated. "In this kind of weather your horses can graze in the meadow over yonder. They'll be perfectly safe there. You'll find plenty of firewood just for the picking up, and the water in the spring in sweet and pure."

"I've heard a little bit about Sierra City, Matt," Jessie said. "Is it true that everybody who lived here got scared one winter when it started to snow and just moved out and never did come back?"

"That's about the size of it." The lumberman nodded. "It just happens I got acquainted with old Snowshoe

Thompson a few years before he died, and he told me the whole story."

"I've heard of Snowshoe Thompson," Jessie said. "He was the man who carried the mail over the Sierras before the railroad was finished. But that was years ago."

"That's right," Bolton said. "He was getting up in years when I ran into him, and about all he could do was yarn by then. But he was real proud that he never missed a trip, even when the snow closed the passes. He even showed me his snowshoes. He'd made them himself. They were kind of funny-looking, more like barrel staves than anything else, only longer and not quite as curved. Had straps in the middle that kept 'em on his feet."

"There must be a lot of snow here in winter, then," Ki remarked.

"It gets right deep, some years," Bolton agreed. "Forty, sometimes even fifty feet."

"And the people who'd moved here got panicky?" Ki asked.

"From what old Snowshoe told me, that was the second year that Sierra City had more people living here than you could count on your fingers," the lumberman replied. "The first year the town got to be any size they had one of those forty-or fifty-foot snows I mentioned a minute ago, and nobody could get in or out of Sierra City. The folks up here like to've starved that winter, Snowshoe said. He couldn't help 'em—all he could manage to carry was his mail sack and supply bag."

When Bolton paused, Jessie asked, "So when it started to snow the second year, they panicked?"

"Something like that." Bolton nodded. "After a few left, it seems like the panic started to spread. All of 'em started to leave, just toting what they could on backpacks. Old Snowshoe said he'd swung around to come through here that year they left, and the snow wasn't really all that deep."

"Did he say how deep it was?" Ki asked.

"Well, he could bend down and look in the second story of the hotel. He said there was a few two-story houses here then, besides the hotel, and he peeped in all the windows. He told me everything in the rooms he looked at was just like folks were still living downstairs, beds all made up, washbowls on the nightstands, all the furniture and carpet, and everything else just like they'd left it."

"And they never came back to get their belongings?" Jessie asked.

"Why, I imagine the ones that settled down in Truckee or Reno or some of the towns close by came back and got what they'd left, Miz Jessie," Bolton answered. "But Snowshoe Thompson said he heard that most of them had moved on back East by the time the snow melted. I'd guess they figured it was cheaper just to buy new things than to travel back here and ship what they'd left to wherever they were living by then. Anyhow, after they left nobody ever wanted to live here again until Clem Harney stumbled onto the place. He told me that was a year or so ago, so he hasn't been here in the Sierras as long as I have."

Jessie nodded, but said nothing. She was wondering how different Alex's life—and consequently her own—would have been if he'd settled on Sierra City for his retreat instead of choosing the Circle Star.

Ki said, "That's a very interesting story, Mr. Bolton. But if Jessie and I are going to pick out one of those houses and stay here to wait for Mr. Harney to get back, we'd better do it before dark." Turning to Jessie, he asked, "We are going to stay, aren't we?"

"It's the easiest thing to do," she said. "Mr. Bolton's right about that. And we'd be better off resting here for a day or two instead of going back to Truckee. Yes, we'll stay."

While he and Jessie were listening to Matt Bolton, Ki had been studying the houses. He pointed to one now and

70

said, "If we're going to stay, then let's start by looking at that place over there. It looks to be in pretty good shape."

"If it's not, there's plenty of others to choose from," Bolton told him. "But I'll leave the choice up to you. When you've picked one out and settled in, I'll be here in the old hotel if you need anything."

"Thank you." Jessie nodded, then turned to Ki. "Let's go and see what that house looks like."

★

Chapter 7

With Ki leading their horses, they walked over to the house and went inside. The shutters at the windows were closed, which made the interior dim, but they could see that in all the windows the small glass panes were intact. The interior of the house had received none of the finishing touches that would have qualified it to be called complete. There was no ceiling, and above the rafters they could see water-stained shingles going up to the roof's ridge line. No interior paneling had been installed. On the walls and between its studs the warped boards of the exterior siding let the pre-sunset light filter through in long, thin horizontal cracks where the outside boards had shrunk as they dried. Nothing had been painted, of course.

Though small, the house was divided into three rooms —tiny bedrooms at each end and a center chamber that served as sitting room, dining room and kitchen. As Bolton had half-promised, the place was furnished with the necessities. The furniture consisted of a bed and chair in each bedroom, and though the beds had no sheets, blankets, or pillows, the mattresses were intact. In the larger center room there was a wood-burning range, an unpainted table, and three chairs. A woodbox stood behind the range, half-filled with split chunks.

There were doors in the walls that separated the rooms, and when Ki opened the window in the back wall of the

73

center room to let some fresh air into the place, they could see the outdoor toilet shanty that stood a short distance behind the house.

"We've stayed in worse places," Jessie commented as she and Ki stood in the center of the main room after a cursory examination of the place. "And at most we'll only be here for a few days, less than a week, I'm sure."

"If it suits you, it suits me," Ki said. "I don't think we'd find that any of the others would be much of an improvement. If we do run across one tomorrow that we like better, we can always move into it without any trouble."

"We'll settle for this one, then," Jessie said. "We'll need a lamp, though, so while you're unsaddling I'll go see if I can get one from our new friend."

"I'll tether the horses behind the house while you're gone, then, and bring the saddlebags in," Ki said. He nodded toward the woodbox and added, "There's plenty of wood for tonight, and I suppose I can borrow an axe and split some more tomorrow. I saw deadfalls at the edges of every meadow we passed, so getting in a supply won't be any problem."

"Good." Jessie nodded. "And while I'm talking to Bolton I'll have him show me where the spring is. A bucket of water's about all we need before we settle in for the night."

When Jessie asked Bolton if there was a spare lamp in the old hotel that she and Ki could use, he smiled and said, "Why, you didn't need to come all the way up here for a lamp, Miz Jessie. Just take one from any of the houses on your way back. If it needs to be filled—" He broke off and said, "Now, there isn't any need to put you to all that trouble. You just take the one sitting on that table across the room there, and I'll go out before dark and pick up another one for myself."

"That's very nice of you," Jessie said as Bolton stepped over to the table and picked up the lamp. When he handed it to her, she went on, "Now, one more thing, and I won't

74

bother you any more. But I need to know where the spring is."

"Right up at the edge of the meadow. But I don't guess you brought a bucket, did you?"

"I'm afraid not."

"Then I'd better give you one." Bolton left the room and returned carrying a tin pail. As he handed it to Jessie he said, "You'll find the water's pure and sweet, like I told you. And if there's anything else you're short of, just let me know and I imagine I can find it for you."

"Thank you, I will. Now, I'd better get back before it's too dark for Ki to find his way to the spring."

Back at their temporary shelter, Jessie handed Ki the bucket and told him where to find the spring. She stood outside the weatherbeaten house and watched as he started up the path Bolton had indicated. Dusk was beginning to shade to darkness now, and the tops of the towering pines on the crest beyond the meadow were outlined in black against the clear sky. A cool wind had begun to blow and was rippling gently across the level hollow in which the house stood.

As Jessie followed Ki with her eyes, she saw a shape moving in the dusk. She watched it for a moment before she could make out the form of a deer ambling past, going toward the meadow. It was a big buck, its wide-spreading antlers visible in the steadily dying light.

Jessie gazed at the deer as it moved along slowly, and it suddenly turned to look directly at her, its eyes glowing with light reflected from the open cabin door. Without thinking, she turned to get a better look at the animal. Slight as her movement was, the deer snorted and leaped away. In a moment it was lost to sight in the tall pines that stood thick around the little clearing. Jessie listened to the small rustlings made by the animal as it pushed through the brush. Then, suddenly at peace with the world, she went into the house and began unpacking her saddlebags.

•   •   •

"I'm afraid the only thing hot that we're going to have for supper tonight is coffee," Jessie told Ki when he returned from the spring carrying a bucket of water.

"You won't get any complaints from me about a cold supper, as long as there's plenty of it," Ki replied.

"Don't worry, there's ham left from the butt we bought when we stopped at Truckee, and enough bread to make sandwiches tonight and have toast for breakfast, but after that we'll have to cook beans."

"There's been plenty of times in the past when we've lived on beans for several days," Ki said as he turned back to face her after placing the bucket of water on the floor behind the stove. "It won't be anything new to do it again. But maybe Bolton can find us something more in Harney's stock tomorrow."

"Right now, a ham sandwich and a cup of hot coffee will do me very well," Jessie said as she filled the small coffeepot with water from the bucket. "While the coffee's brewing, I'm going to make up my bed. After a full day of riding over these mountains, I'm beginning to feel sleepy."

"I don't suppose you have any preferences about the bedrooms, do you?" Ki asked.

"Not a bit. Just throw my blanket roll in one and yours in the other. As soon as I've eaten a sandwich and had some coffee, I'm going to bed."

"It's the altitude that's making us both sleepy," Ki said. "We have the same thing happen every time we leave the Circle Star and go into high country. But I'm as ready for bed as you are. We'll turn in as soon as we've eaten, then. By tomorrow, we'll be a little bit better adjusted to this nine-thousand-foot height."

"Well, where do we start now?" Ki asked.

He and Jessie were standing as close as possible to the kitchen stove, which was just beginning to radiate heat into the chilly morning air that had crept in overnight through

76

the cracks between the boards of the walls and around the loosely fitting windows and doors.

"I intend to start by staying right here by the stove until this place is comfortably warm," Jessie replied. "The minute I got out of bed this morning, I began getting cold. The air up here in the Sierras certainly isn't as comfortable as it is at home on the Circle Star."

"I've noticed that myself." Ki smiled. "But I suppose we'll get used to it in a few days."

"A few days is all I'd planned to stay," Jessie reminded him. "We'll start back home as soon as we can stop this Harney fellow from using Alex's name to lure innocent victims into his net."

"You know, Jessie, it might be easier to say that than to do it," Ki said soberly.

"That's what I was thinking myself last night after I'd gone to bed," she replied. "But that's what we came up here to do, and I suppose there's enough of Alex's stubborness in me to make me stick to the job until I've finished it."

"I'm not suggesting you give up," Ki said. "You know that, of course. Suppose we see what kind of plan we can come up with while we eat breakfast."

For the first few minutes after sitting down, Jessie and Ki both shivered occasionally as they ate the hot toast and cold ham and drank warmed-over coffee without speaking. By the time they'd finished breakfast, the stove had done its work in banishing the chill that night had brought into the cabin.

Going back to the topic they'd been discussing before breakfast, Jessie said, "I've been trying to think of ways we can prove that this Clem Harney is running a confidence game, Ki, but I keep running into the fact that so far we haven't a bit of evidence he is. All we've been going on is a hunch."

"You'll have the evidence you want if Harney offers you

some kind of preposterous proposition when he gets back and you start talking to him," Ki pointed out.

"But if he doesn't, or if he's very careful about what he promises, there won't be anything we can do except face him outright and tell him I want him to stop using the Starbuck name. After that, we'll just have to play it by ear."

"I don't think Harney would listen to a plain request." Ki frowned. "My guess is that a bigger threat will be needed to move him."

"Jail?" Jessie suggested. "He'd more than likely be convicted of fraud if I filed a bunco charge against him in the court at Truckee."

"Don't be too sure. He'd defend himself by saying he wasn't breaking the law. Technically, he'd be right, I think. Remember, Jessie, the law here in California favors the miner over the landowner. The judge would have to rule that Harney's lease is still valid if he can show just an ounce or two of gold that came off this land he leased from Alex."

"Law or no law, he's got to be stopped!" Jessie said firmly.

"Oh, I agree with you," Ki said. "But don't let your feelings about Alex overcome your good judgment."

"I don't intend to. But somewhere along the line we'll be able to dig up the evidence we need."

"We might be overlooking a good source of evidence," Ki suggested. "Matt Bolton seems to know a great deal about Harney and what he's been doing. Harney wouldn't leave him here alone to look after things if he didn't trust him."

"He wouldn't be likely to confide in us, though. We've just met him," Jessie pointed out.

"I can't think of a better time than now, while Harney's still gone, to get to know him better," Ki said.

"Now that you've mentioned Bolton, I'm wondering if he and Harney might not be working together," Jessie said. "And I think that finding out might be the best first step we can take." She sat silently thoughtful for a moment, then went on, "I'll make it my business to find out, Ki. And since we haven't any idea when Harney's going to get back, I'd better start at once."

"Harney might be back any time," Ki agreed. "If we have a little bit of ammunition, we'll be a lot better off. And while you're talking to Bolton, I'll have a look around. In case we run into problems, we'd better know a little bit about the area here."

"Good idea. I'll see you here about noon, then. While I'm talking to Bolton I'll find out what we can get from Harney's storeroom to add to the food we brought along."

Jessie walked between the rows of deserted houses to the big, two-story structure that had been Sierra City's hotel. The door was open, and she could see Bolton sitting at a table in the big room that had obviously been the hotel lobby. She tapped lightly on the doorjamb, and Bolton looked around.

"Why, just walk right on in, Miz Jessie," he said. "And I hope you'll excuse me if I don't stand up, but I've got to keep holding on to my work here or it'll be ruined."

"Don't interrupt whatever you're doing on my account," Jessie told him as she crossed the room to the table where he sat. "I just stopped by to—" She stopped short, staring at the miscellany of objects strewn on the tabletop, and asked, "Please forgive my curiosity, but what on earth are you doing?"

Spools of varicolored wood, silk thread, bits of fur, an assortment of rainbow-hued feathers of different sizes, a small bottle of some kind of liquid, and a number of little boxes filled with fishhooks lay scattered on the tabletop. A pair of tiny scissors and a lump of what appeared to be putty lay near the edge in front of Bolton, where a rod of metal, bent to an upward slant, was fixed to the tabletop by a U-shaped strip of metal. At the angled tip of the rod was a fishhook wrapped with thread. The thread led to a spool that Bolton was holding in one hand.

"I'm making a few fly hooks," the logger replied. "Had an idea I might go out fishing later on."

"How can you use hooks wrapped up in thread to fish with?" Jessie asked. "I thought you had to have bait of some kind."

"Most people do. They're wrong, though. Fish—especially trout in these mountain lakes and streams—eat insects that land on the top of the water. The trick is to dabble one of these artificial insects on the surface and make the trout think it's real. Then he'll come up and grab it, and if you can play him a while until he's tired without breaking your leader you can land him, and—well, fresh-fried trout makes about the best meal I can think of."

"I've never heard of such a thing!" Jessie exclaimed. "You aren't just spinning me a tall tale, are you?"

"Not at all," Bolton replied. "Here, just let me finish this fly hook while you watch, and maybe you'll see how much it looks like a real insect."

While Jessie watched, Bolton selected a wisp from one of the strands of flossy silk. His fingers moved with a delicacy Jessie had not dreamed of associating with such a practical man in such a place as he wound the yellow silken strands onto the thread-covered hook and held it in place with a loop of thread while he trimmed off the excess material.

He picked up a thin, wispy feather no longer than Jessie's finger and, in some manner that she did not quite understand, curled it around the fishhook so that the fibers spread and formed a bushy circle below the hook's eye. Taking the scissors, he trimmed off the tip of the feather that remained, then added several more wrappings of thread before looping it off below the hook's eye. Dexterously, he cut the thread off close to the hook's eye, freeing it from the hook, and motioned for Jessie to bend over for a closer look.

"If I hadn't watched you do that, I wouldn't have believed it was possible," she said. "But it does look something like an insect, I suppose."

"It does when it's floating on the surface of the water," Bolton assured her. "At least it looks enough like an insect to fool a trout."

"But how do you get it out on the water where the fish will see it?" Jessie asked.

Bolton swiveled in his chair and leaned back, looking at Jessie with raised eyebrows. "With a line and rod, of course," he said, and when he saw that Jessie was still at sea he asked, "Miz Jessie, haven't you ever done any fishing?"

Shaking her head, Jessie replied, "No. Never."

"Do you mind telling me where you're from?"

"Of course not. I live on a ranch in the southwestern part of Texas."

"That would explain it, then." The logger nodded. "I don't guess there's much water there?"

"Very little that doesn't come from a well, or collect in low spots on the prairie when it rains. There are a few springs, but we usually make stock ponds out of them."

Now it was Bolton's turn to frown questioningly. "Stock ponds?" he repeated.

"Pools of water where cattle can drink," Jessie explained.

"And I don't suppose there are any fish in the ponds?"

"Why, of course not! Oh, there are fish in the rivers, but there aren't any rivers that flow across my ranch. Even if there were, I don't suppose there'd be fish in them."

"They might surprise you." Bolton smiled. "But I don't imagine they'd be trout like we have up here in the mountains."

"All I know about trout is that I order them from the menu at restaurants," Jessie confessed. "But are you telling me that the little hook you just put that thread and feathers on will really catch a fish?"

"It certainly will," Bolton assured her. "And if you don't have anything else to do at the moment, I'd be glad for you to stroll up to the lake at the top of the meadow and let me prove it to you."

Jessie realized at once that she'd found a soft spot in Bolton's makeup that would give her an opportunity to combine questioning him about Clem Harney with satisfying her own curiosity about fishing.

"If you have the time..." she said, letting her words trail off into silence.

"I haven't anything but time," he told her. "Fishing with an artificial fly is my hobby. When work on my logging stand is tapering off the way it is right now, I take the chance to try my luck at fooling the trout in the lake up here."

"You've cut all the trees on the land you're logging?" she asked.

"No, of course not. There'll be plenty of trees left, but they'll be small ones. We only cut the biggest. That gives the younger trees a chance to mature. But now that we're getting close to clearing out the merchantable timber, I can let my foremen look after things while I take a few days off to enjoy a little bit of fishing."

Jessie started to tell Bolton that she knew a great deal more about logging than she did about fishing. Before she could speak, though, she realized that if she mentioned the Starbuck timbering operations in the Pacific Northwest she'd be opening the way to questions that might destroy her pose as an innocent potential customer of Clem Harney's who'd come to Sierra City to investigate buying a gold claim in the Sierras. She quickly switched the subject back to fishing.

"I'd enjoy going with you," she said. "You've got my curiosity aroused, because I can't really believe you can catch a fish with that little bug you made. How do you get it out on the water where the fish are?"

"Let me get my rod and creel and I'll show you," he told her. "I can explain it all while we're walking up to the lake."

★

Chapter 8

Bolton stood up and stepped to the corner of the room. He groped for a moment, then started back, carrying a long, thin fishing rod fitted with arched wire guides and a large wooden reel at the bottom, below a grip shaped like an oversized cigar. In the other hand he carried an oddly shaped basket made of woven willow twigs.

"Come on outside," he said. "I'll show you how this rod works, then you'll understand."

Jessie followed him outside, and Bolton put down his basket and took the rod by the grip.

"This is the latest thing in fishing rods," he told her as he threaded the line through the guides. "I ordered it from a man named Hardy, in England. He's invented a way to make rods out of bamboo by cutting it in strips, then gluing them together. This odd-looking piece of line is the leader. It's made out of silkworm gut and comes from China." Knotting on the fly he'd just finished making, he went on, "Now watch, and you'll see how all this comes together."

Taking the rod by its grip, Bolton raised it until its tip was vertical, then brought it forward with a sharp snapping motion. The line, which had been dangling loose, shot forward in a straight line and dropped to the ground. He repeated the snapping move after pulling more line from the reel, and again the line shot forward, the fly at its end landing a good fifteen or twenty feet from where he and Jessie stood.

"Why, that's astonishing!" Jessie exclaimed. "I can understand now. When you're standing on the edge of a lake, you can get your fly way out on the water, can't you?"

"Exactly." Bolton nodded. "Now let's walk on up to the lake and see if I can get a fish to take that fly I just tied."

As they started walking up the faint trail that led to the lake, Jessie remarked, "You're a man of many talents, it seems, Matt. Have you always been a lumberman?"

"Pretty much. My father was a forty-niner who made a lot of money and then went broke. I had to leave school to support my mother, and when she died some years ago, I started wandering. Somehow, I got into a logging crew and learned the ropes of the trade, so I stuck with it until I'd earned enough to strike out on my own."

"And you still are? By that I mean, you're not partners with Clem Harney?"

"No, indeed. I'm only interested in Clem for one reason. He has all this good timberland up here, with a lot of good stands of mature pine, and I want to lease it for logging. It's close to the stand I'll be closing down in another month or two, so it'd be easy for me to bring my crew up here and start them working without any lost time."

"I see." Jessie nodded. "He must own a lot of land around here, then."

"He's never told me how much," Bolton said. "But from what I've been able to find out, it takes in quite a lot of good timber stands."

"Wouldn't gold mining and cutting timber interfere with one another on the same land?"

Bolton shook his head. "Not a bit. In fact, if this does develop into mining land it'd help us both. I could supply the miners with wood from what I'm wasting now, and they'd be free to put all their time into mining instead of cutting firewood and so on."

"Yes, I can see that," Jessie said.

"I've asked Harney several times about getting timber rights up here, but he keeps stalling me," Bolton went on. "In fact, I'm—" He broke off as they pushed through the narrow strip of low-growing brush that stood a bit away from the water's edge and then said, "Well, that's neither here nor there. Let's see if the fly I just tied will bring us a fish. If I show you how to make a cast, would you like to try your hand at it?"

"Me?" Jessie asked in surprise. "I've already told you, I don't know the first thing about fishing!"

"It's never too late to learn," Bolton said. "Now come down to the edge of the water and I'll show you how to cast this outfit."

Still too surprised to protest, Jessie walked with Bolton to the water's edge. He put the rod in Jessie's hand and guided her arm with his own hand to show her the motion she needed to make. To her surprise, the fly sailed out over the water and settled down on its surface twenty or more feet from shore. Her eyes wide, Jessie was turning to Bolton to ask him what to do next when a splash broke the surface of the placid blue water and the line suddenly drew taut.

"What happened?" Jessie asked, looking at the line, which was moving at a slant toward the center of the lake.

"You've hooked a trout, that's what happened," Bolton replied with a wide grin. "Now just do what I tell you, and we'll get that fellow in here to shore!"

By now the line had tightened and Jessie felt the tugging of the invisible trout. The tip of the rod was arcing into a curve, and line was running off the reel. She looked at Bolton, her face showing her bewilderment.

"What do I do?" she asked. "The fish is going to break that thin little line in a minute!"

"Just let him run," Bolton said. "He'll pull line off the reel, but don't worry about that. He'll stop pretty soon, then you'll want to turn the knob on the reel to keep your line tight. Just don't put too much pressure on it."

In a moment the line sagged and grew slack, and Jessie could no longer feel the trout's tugs.

"Crank the reel a turn or two," Bolton told her. "Just enough to tighten the line. Don't turn it too fast—just slow and easy."

Jessie began turning the reel handle, and after several revolutions the line grew taut and she could once again feel the fish tugging at it. Then the trout lunged. She was unprepared for its quick response, which pulled the rod's tip into an arc once more as the line cut through the water.

"Let go of the reel, quick!" Bolton urged. "He wants to run again!"

Before Jessie could release the reel's knobby handle the lake's placid surface broke as the trout jumped. The fish seemed to explode from the blue water into the air, and Jessie gave a small gasp of surprise when she glimpsed its gleaming sides, irridescent in the sunshine. Still in midair, it bent into a shining arc as it started to fall, then it hit the water with another splash and disappeared. Belatedly, she remembered to release the reel handle and it spun wildly as the fish ran.

"He's sure hooked solid!" Bolton said. "Now all you have to do is keep a tight line, and you've got him."

Jessie's quick mind had already grasped the basic technique, and a bit of experimenting showed her how to follow the taut line with the tip of the arced rod as the trout raced back and forth underwater, parallel to the bank. When its moves grew slower, Bolton again began his instructions.

"Start reeling in now," he said. "Easy, though. Don't use any more pressure than you need just to keep the line tight."

Her muscles' reflexes were honed sharp by the active

life she led, and Jessie had no trouble following Bolton's instructions. She kept her hand on the knob of the reel, and when the rod's tip bent in response to the trout's struggles, she let the line slip through the guides to ease the pressure. The pulsing moves of the hooked trout began to fascinate her, and instinctively she let it take line until it tired, then reeled in against the fish's diminishing tugs.

Soon she could see the trout's sides shining through the clear water as it came closer to shore. The fish was very tired now, the strength of its lunges diminishing rapidly. After a few moments, as Jessie kept the line taut, the trout turned on its side and she could glimpse its gills working furiously under the inch or so of water that now covered it.

"It's a good one!" Bolton said enthusiastically. "Just keep your line tight and you've got him!"

"But how do I get it on the bank?" Jessie asked. "That line at the end is so thin I'm afraid it'll break!"

"Likely it would," Bolton agreed. "But don't worry, I'll take care of landing it."

Without stopping to take off his calf-high logger's boots he waded out a half-dozen feet into the lake. Jessie grasped his intention, and swung the rod's tip slowly to bring the trout closer to him. When the fish was within a few inches of Bolton's legs, he bent down quickly, cupping his hands as he closed them below the fish. Then, with a sudden move, he lifted the trout and tossed it to shore near Jessie's feet.

Jessie did not really notice when the line slackened and the rod sprung straight, she was too engrossed in watching the trout as it flopped around and arched its body, trying to reach the water again. Bolton had started wading to shore when he tossed the fish, and he reached the squirming trout before it could flop back into the lake.

Picking up the trout by its tail, he twisted the hook out of its jaw. Then he held up one of his booted feet and brought the fish down against the edge of his thick boot sole to break its neck. The trout was dead when its spine snapped, but it quivered for a moment before going limp. Bolton held it out to Jessie.

"It's your fish," he said. "You hooked it and played it and brought it in. It's a nice one, close to three pounds. I'll clean it, then you and Ki can have it for supper."

"Oh, no!" Jessie protested. "I couldn't take it. After all, I caught it with your pole and you told me what to do before I landed it."

"That doesn't make any difference. When you catch a trout, it's your fish. That's—" He broke off as a splash sounded from the lake. He and Jessie both looked across the water and saw the widening ring left by the leaping trout a dozen yards from the shore. "They're moving now," Bolton went on. "I'll tell you what. Suppose I see if I can take another one, then if you think you can put up with me, I'll join you and Ki for supper."

"We've got a deal." Jessie nodded. "Go ahead."

When Jessie did not return after he'd waited for what seemed to be a long time, Ki stepped to the door and looked toward the old hotel. He saw Jessie and Bolton starting toward the lake, and frowned thoughtfully.

"Jessie must have some good reason for going with Bolton," he told himself. "And he's carrying a fishing rod, so it looks like she's going with him to the lake while he fishes. Maybe she stumbled onto something, maybe she didn't. Either way, it'd be a mistake to join her and Bolton, and waiting here for her to come back would be a waste of time. So I'll see if I can find any useful information by looking somewhere else."

Glancing around, Ki saw the signs of trails leading in four directions. He and Jessie had come into Sierra City on the wide, well-beaten road from the east, and had gotten a look at the Starbuck property in that direction. Now Ki was faced with making a choice. He could go downslope toward Bolton's logging stand, up the slope that rose north of the lake, or follow the old road still further to the northwest, spiraling up the flanks of the Sierras.

Whichever direction he chose would give him an opportunity to look at part of the land being offered by Clem Harney for mining claims, Ki realized. With a shrug, he turned and headed down the slope.

For the first half or three-quarters of a mile, Ki walked through a forest that was still virgin, untouched by the axe and saw of the logger. With Jessie, Ki had visited the Starbuck timber holdings enough times to recognize what he was seeing, and he also recognized the forestland that had been cut over when he came to the end of the untouched forest and crossed the line marked by yellow-topped stumps that showed loggers had recently been at work.

Behind him there were majestic pines with boles three times the diameter of a man's chest, towering above the whitethorn and azalea and trapper's tea bushes. There were still pine trees on the downslope ahead, but they were small by comparison.

On the rise behind him, the boles of the pines could be encircled by a man's arms, and stood widely separated. The undergrowth that was so thick in the area Ki had just left was replaced by small, young shoots in the area that stretched in front of him. Underfoot the duff from which they sprouted was thin, scored in deep furrows where the butts of tree trunks had been dragged, and beside the furrows it was pocked by the hoofprints of the oxteams that had hauled the logs away.

Between the deep furrows the earth did not feel softly spongy now, but was firm and hard and dry underfoot. Around the stumps it was littered with big yellow chips and small, browning, dry branches from the trees that had recently been felled and trimmed into logs. Overhead the sky was visible now, no longer hidden by sweeping branches. Big patches of sunlight made bright puddles on the ground, and the vista ahead was now a partly open one. After he'd walked on a few yards, Ki could see bright flashes of sunshine dancing from running water a short distance ahead, and he changed his course toward the little stream that coursed down the slope between the trees that still remained untouched.

There were enough trees left to prevent Ki from seeing very far ahead as he changed his course and started toward the stream. He moved ahead slowly, realizing that he was no longer on Starbuck land, but curious to see what lay beyond. After he'd covered a short distance he reached the running creek that had caught his eye when he was higher on the slope. The creek was very shallow, only inches deep, and its water was glass-clear. Ki hunkered down beside it and cupped his hand to dip water and drink a swallow or two.

As Ki stood up after drinking he looked along the bed of the little creek and saw that he'd reached a ledge where the ground dropped off sharply. Some distance past the ledge he saw a thin line of smoke rising. Telling himself that he must be close to Matt Bolton's lumber camp, and curious to see what it looked like, Ki walked on to the edge of the drop-off, where the stream plunged straight down several feet in a miniature waterfall.

Though the drop-off was steep, almost perpendicular, it was only six or seven feet high. Ki jumped off it, landed with the smooth, resilient spring with which a cat might end a leap, and continued walking along the edge of the brook. There was less slant to the ground below the ledge and more brush along the banks of the creek here, and in the distance he could see an area of bright sunshine that marked the spread of a mountain meadow.

Though the loggers had cleared the forest of its bigger trees, there were still enough smaller pines left standing to hide the ground around the spot where the smoke-thread rose. Ki could tell that its source was at one side of the meadow, but he could see no buildings in the area visible through the trees. He walked on, his attention more on the smoke than on the stream he was following. Suddenly a soft laugh broke the silence. Ki stopped, his eyes searching the ground between the trees on each side of the stream, but he saw no signs of movement.

Startled by the laugh, and very curious as to its source, Ki began moving along the bank of the stream once more. The patchy waterside growth of azaleas mixed with whitethorn was thicker here, spreading from the water's edge into the trees for fifteen or twenty feet in places, and growing with such density that Ki was forced to detour around them. He'd made one such detour—the third or fourth since resuming his walk—when he heard the liquid purling laugh again, but this time it was coming from behind him.

Turning, Ki covered the short distance to the edge of the stream with three long steps. He got a blurred glimpse of white skin as he pushed through the screening brush, then as he got his first unobstructed view of the creek his jaw dropped and his eyes opened wider than usual.

A young woman, covered only by the strands of long blond hair that fell over her shoulders, sat in the middle of the creek. Her arms were outstretched, her hands paddling in the clear water. She looked calmly at Ki, her full lips curled in a small smile, her oval face calmly serene.

"What—what on earth are you doing here?" Ki stammered.

"Taking a bath," she replied calmly. "Don't you bathe?"

"Of course. But not in a place like this."

"You'd bathe in a place like this too, if it was the only place you had," she said. "Besides, I like it here. It's close and the water isn't too cold."

"Close?" Ki frowned. "Close to what?"

"Why, to where I live. Don't you know?"

"I'm afraid I don't," Ki told her. "Just exactly where do you live?"

She waved toward a closely spaced stand of small pines that stood a hundred yards or more away, across the little watercourse from the bank where Ki was standing.

"There," she said.

Following her gesture with his eyes, Ki now saw the gleam of raw pine boards between the trees in the pine stand. As nearly as he could make out, the boards formed the walls of a small cabin, almost totally concealed by the trunks of the closely spaced trees that grew around it. Ki's bewilderment was growing minute by minute, but during his career as a wanderer and later as Alex Starbuck's and Jessie's trusted aide, he'd encountered many strange things.

"Who lives there with you?" he asked, still trying to fathom the mystery of the young woman.

"Nobody. That's why I like it."

"Where are you from?" Ki asked.

"From? Why, from nowhere. I live here, except when the snow's too deep. Then Uncle Matt takes me with him."

"Matt Bolton?"

"Of course. He's the only uncle I have."

"Does he live there with you?"

"No! He knows I don't like anybody living with me."

"I guess I don't understand," Ki told her, shaking his head in bewilderment. "How do you manage to live alone here in the mountains? What do you do for food?"

"Why, the men bring me food. So does Uncle Matt."

"What men?"

"All of them do, when they come to visit me."

Ki wondered if his first thought when he heard the girl's words were correct, but quickly decided that he'd better wait until later to pursue the line of questioning that came to his mind. Instead he asked, "I guess you have a name?"

"Yes, of course. I'm Ariane."

"Ariane what?"

"Just Ariane. Who are you?"

"My name is Ki."

"Hello, Ki."

"Hello, Ariane," Ki replied. He was still bewildered, but he'd encountered stranger situations.

"Were you looking for me?" Ariane asked.

Ki shook his head. "No. Why?"

"Because they usually are, when they don't find me at home."

"They? Who's they?"

"Why, the men who cut the trees, of course. But you're not one of them, I can tell that now."

"No."

Ariane shook her head and raised her hands to push her long blond hair down her back, then to Ki's surprise she stood up. Her wet body glistened in the filtered sunlight, and except for the pink pebbled rosettes of her full breasts and a wisp of almost invisible blond pubic curls she might have been a marble statue carved by some master sculptor.

"You can help me rub dry," she said. "Then I'll be ready to go to the cabin with you."

Chapter 9

Although after Ariane's casual display of her nude body Ki understood perfectly why she was inviting him to her cabin, he stalled her.

"Why do you want me to go with you?" he asked.

"Didn't you come up here to find me?" Ariane asked as she started wading toward the shore.

"No. I didn't even know you lived here."

Ariane had reached the bank of the stream now. She stepped onto the shore and walked up to Ki. At close range, she was even more attractive. Her body was without a blemish, though the chill of the water had pebbled her milky skin into small goose bumps. Several strands of her long golden hair were clinging to her shoulders, and she tossed her head to free them before raising her hands to push them down her back again.

Looking at Ki, she said, "Will you help rub me dry? The air is cold."

Ki hesitated for a moment, then nodded. "Of course."

Ariane edged closer to Ki and turned her back to him. "You can rub my back where I can't reach," she said, beginning to stroke her shoulders and breasts with her palms. "When I'm dry, I won't be so cold."

Ki lifted the long golden strands that hung down below her shoulders and began rubbing her back briskly with the palm of his free hand. Ariane finished removing the drops of water from her shoulders and bulging breasts and moved her hands down to her ribs. Ki finished patting the strands of her golden hair between his palms to remove the excess water that had been dripping from them and, as she lowered her hands to her stomach and bent her head to follow their movements, he draped the partly dried hair over her shoulders to get it out of his way while he rubbed away the drops that still clung to her shoulder blades.

As Ariane bent still farther forward the lubricious feeling of the slippery, smooth skin of her back as the friction of his palms warmed it began working on Ki. He felt an erection starting, and though he normally kept his body under firm control, this time he found to his surprise and chagrin that he could not suppress the swelling. Even when he used the entire force of his mind trying to halt the bulging it continued, and by the time his hands reached the inward taper of Ariane's waist he was fully and uncomfortably erect.

As Ki touched the softer flesh of Ariane's hips and the beginning softness of her rounding buttocks his urge grew more intense, until at last he abandoned his efforts at control. He let his tumescence take over as he stroked the firm but yielding mounds and dropped to one knee to remove the trickles of water that were now running down the backs of her thighs.

Ariane was bending forward now, spreading her legs as she stroked them with cupped palms. As she parted her thighs Ki glimpsed the thin golden haze of her water-matted brush and decided that she could finished her rubdown without his help. He stood up and stepped away from her. Ariane stroked her other leg, then straightened up and turned to face him.

"I feel better now." She smiled. "Warm and nice."

Her eyes dropped to Ki's crotch, and her smile grew wider as she saw the bulge in his loosely fitting trousers. Before he grasped her intention, she had her hands on his swelling shaft and was fondling and squeezing him.

"Oh, my," she went on. "We'd better go to my cabin now. I don't like the ground any more. It's too rough."

Ki grasped Ariane's wrists and as gently as possible moved her hands away from him. She gazed into his eyes, her own eyes puzzled, a small frown flitting across her face.

"Don't you like me?" she asked in a small, worried voice.

"I like you very much, Ariane," Ki replied. "But I didn't come looking for you to go to bed with you."

"Why not? All the men do." Ariane's tone was quite matter-of-fact.

"But I didn't even know you were here," Ki protested. "I was just out for a walk, to look at the scenery."

"But wouldn't you like to go to bed with me? All the others do. And I like it, too. Going to bed with somebody and making them feel good makes me feel good."

"I understand that, Ariane," Ki said. "But—" He came to a stop while he racked his brain. Almost from the first moment they'd begun talking he'd seen that Ariane lived on the thin borderline that divides sanity from unreality.

Ki had come to maturity in the Orient, where the code of morality and the general attitude toward sex was far more relaxed than that of the Anglo-Saxon nations. He understood Jessie's occasional flings and found nothing wrong with them, and he looked on his own dalliances in the same way.

However, very early during his career with Alex he'd come to understand and respect the differences in attitude between the land of his birth and his adopted country. While he was sure that Matt Bolton must know of Ariane's casual attitude toward sex, he was far from sure that Matt approved of it. Before he could make up his mind how to respond to her casual invitation she saved him from having to choose.

"Of course, you don't have to," Ariane told him. "Maybe you're like Uncle Matt. He doesn't go to bed with me, either."

"I suppose I must be like him, then." Ki nodded. "Just the same, I think you're very nice, and maybe we'll have another talk later on."

"All right. I do like to talk to people, and there aren't many others out here in the woods."

"You'd better put on your clothes and go back to your cabin, then," Ki told her.

"My dress is at my cabin," she said. "I don't like dresses very much, so I don't wear one unless it's cold."

"Then you'd better hurry to your cabin and put it on, and I'll move along. But we'll talk again, I'm sure."

"All right," Ariane said. "Because I am getting too cold now. But come back again when you want to, Ki."

With a smile, Ariane turned to wade across the stream. For a moment, Ki watched the glimmer of her white body and golden hair as she made her way toward the cabin. Then he turned and started back to Sierra City.

"This fish I took's not as big as yours, but the two of them ought to make a pretty good supper for the three of us," Bolton said as he dropped the two fish on the table in the house where Jessie and Ki were staying.

"They certainly will, Matt," Jessie agreed. "But I don't know when Ki will be coming back, so I won't start cooking until he shows up, then I'll get him to call you."

"That'll be fine," Bolton replied. "I don't have anything much to do, just stay here and look after things till Clem gets back. And I sure hope I can get him to say yes about the timber lease I want."

"Of course, it isn't any of my business," Jessie said. "But if you two are as friendly as you seem to be, why is Mr. Harney holding back?"

"That's something I can't figure out, Miz Jessie." Bolton frowned. "You know, ever since I saw that I was getting close to the end of cleaning up that stand I've got down the slope, I started asking Clem about a lease up here. But he just keeps putting me off."

"It seems to me that it'd be a lot easier for you just to move my gear and lumberjacks up here instead of looking a long way," Jessie said.

"Sure it would," Bolton agreed. "As a matter of fact, it would save me several thousand dollars if I could just move my gear and lumberjacks up here instead of looking for a new stand and maybe finding one a long ways off. But—well, maybe Clem will come around when I talk to him after he gets back."

"I think you said he'd be back soon?"

"He oughta be. I imagine you'd like to get your business with him settled, too."

"Of course. But I'm a bit surprised to find that there isn't anybody else here. It seems to me that whoever has a gold claim up here would be working to make it pay off."

"For all I know, there could be a dozen claims being worked right now," Bolton said. "But if there are, I haven't heard Clem talking about them. I know he's sold some claims upslope from here, and I guess the folks who bought 'em are working 'em."

"But he hasn't mentioned how much gold they're finding?"

"Not to me. And I don't spend much time here, except like now, when he gets me to keep an eye on things."

"He owns the land, I suppose?" Jessie asked, keeping her voice carefully casual.

"As far as I know, he does. He talks like he does, calls it his place and things like that. But outside of that timber lease I'm after, we haven't talked business very much. I'm not one to pry into another man's affairs."

"Then you don't have any part in his gold-mining venture?"

"Not a bit. Lumberjacking is my trade, Miz Jessie. It's the only one I know, and I've got sense enough not to branch out into something I don't know the first thing about."

Thinking of her own problems right after Alex's death and the trouble she'd had mastering his far-flung business ventures, Jessie nodded and said, "I see you've given it quite a bit of thought."

"Well, sure. Logging's hard work, but it pays good. But even if I felt different, Clem has never asked me if I was interested in throwing in with him. I'm glad enough to oblige him by coming up here for a few days to keep an eye on this place while he's gone, and he helps me out by picking up stuff I need from San Francisco or Los Angeles, whichever one he happens to be going to. Besides, outside of a couple of little creeks that run through my logging stand, that lake out there's the only place close by for me to fish."

"I can understand why men enjoy fishing now," Jessie said. "I certainly did enjoy catching that trout."

While she was talking, Bolton moved to the window and glanced at the sky, then went on, "It's getting on for late. I tell you what, Miz Jessie, while we're waiting for your man Ki to come back, I'll just step up to the hotel and put on some dry pants and shoes."

"Fine." Jessie nodded. "I'll stir up the fire and get the stove good and hot, but I'll wait until both you and Ki are here before starting to cook the trout."

"I guess you do know how to cook 'em, don't you?"

"If I don't, Ki will show me. He's really a much better cook than I am."

"I'll go along and change, then. It won't take but a minute."

Bolton had been gone only a few moments when Ki came in.

"It's too bad you didn't get here a few minutes earlier," Jessie told him. "We're having fish for supper, and Matt Bolton is going to eat with us. He just left to go up to the hotel and put on some dry boots. The ones he was wearing got wet while we were fishing."

"Yes, I saw him walking up to the old hotel," Ki said. "But perhaps it's just as well that he's not here right now."

"Why on earth—" Jessie began.

"Wait, Jessie," Ki broke in. "Purely by accident, I've found out something that's both interesting and puzzling. There's a young woman living in a cabin down on Bolton's logging stand. She claims to be Bolton's niece. A very attractive girl, too, but not quite normal."

"Maybe you'd better explain that a bit better," she suggested.

"Retarded is the best word, I suppose," Ki told her. "Her name's Ariane, by the way. She was bathing in a little creek that runs down the slope. Naked, of course, but that didn't seem to bother her a bit."

"Well, it's hard to take a bath fully dressed." Jessie smiled. "But I can tell there's something else about her that's bothering you. What is it, Ki?"

"She—well, I'll be polite and say that she services the loggers. What puzzles me is that Bolton seems to approve of it."

"That doesn't sound like Matt's style at all!" Jessie exclaimed. "I just can't visualize him operating a whorehouse—which is what this would amount to."

Ki nodded. "It's about the only way you could describe it, even if there is only the one girl involved."

"It's a totally confusing idea, Ki," Jessie said, frowning. "I found Matt to be a nice, thoughtful man while we were fishing up in the lake today."

"It'd be expecting too much for him to have told you about Ariane, of course, but she didn't make any secret of what she's doing. She even invited me to join her in her cabin."

"You didn't, I'm sure."

Ki shook his head. "No. It didn't seem to be the thing for me to do, considering her mental condition."

101

"There's only one thing I can see to do, Ki," Jessie said. "Matt will be back here pretty soon. Let's ask him to tell us what the situation is."

"Do you think he'll tell us the truth?"

"That's a very good question," Jessie replied thoughtfully. "And speaking of questions, I asked Matt about his connection with Clem Harney. I'm satisfied from what he told me that he hasn't anything to do with Harney's business dealings."

"After what I ran into, I wonder if he was telling you the truth."

"My feeling is that he was, Ki," Jessie replied unhesitatingly. "You and I have met enough lying scoundrels during our fights with the cartel so that neither of us can be deceived very easily."

"Then when Bolton gets back, let's just ask him outright," Ki agreed. "I'm sure he couldn't fool both of us."

Matt Bolton himself put an end to the discussion between Jessie and Ki by rapping at the door, then coming in before his knock was answered. He nodded to Ki, then turned to Jessie.

"I brought a few slices of bacon," he said. "Didn't know whether you had any, and bacon grease is the only kind of fat that gets hot enough to cook a trout in."

"Suppose we wait just a minute before we start them cooking," Jessie suggested. "Ki's been looking at your logging stand, Matt, and something happened that's disturbed both of us. I'll admit it isn't any of our business, but—"

"Hold on," Bolton broke in. "From the way you've started out, I've got a pretty good idea that Ki must have run into Ariane."

"I did." Ki nodded.

"Then you know she's not quite right in her head," Bolton said. "Not in a dangerous way, but—well, it's a crazy sort of story, but I think maybe you'll understand when I tell you why I had to bring her up here with me."

"Go ahead," Jessie told him. "We're listening."

"I can guess at what Ki's found out," Bolton began. Without waiting for Ki to do more than nod, he went on, "Ariane's my sister's baby, so I've got to be responsible for her."

"Your sister?" Jessie frowned. "Where is she?"

"Dead and buried more'n twenty years now, Miz Jessie. Marianne—my sister—didn't live but a few hours after Ariane was born. The last thing she said before she died was to ask me to promise I'd look after her baby girl."

"How can you call what you're letting her do looking after her?" Jessie asked.

"Because it's the only way I've found that I can look after her," Bolton replied. "You see, when I promised Marianne, she didn't know, of course, and I didn't either, that Ariane would turn out not to be quite right in the head. But even if I'd known what I was letting myself into, I'd've done the same."

"That's understandable," Jessie put in when Bolton paused. "Go ahead, Matt."

"Sure. Even if it's not easy for me to talk about it." He went on, "Ariane seemed to be all right until she was fifteen. That was six years ago. I was leaving her at home during the summer while I came up here to the Sierras to cut timber. Had a woman come in and live with her while I was gone, but that didn't work out. Ariane was too much for her to handle, or for me to handle, either."

"You mean she suddenly became insane?" Jessie asked when Bolton paused.

He nodded. "Crazy for men, if you'll excuse me saying it so plain, Miz Jessie. I tried putting her away in a crazy house when I had to start my summer work the next year, but when I got back and found out how they'd treated her in that place, I swore I'd never do that again. So I took her with me the next summer. That was when I found out I couldn't control her, either. I just couldn't watch her close enough to keep her from—well, I couldn't blame it all on

103

my lumberjacks, and I couldn't keep her locked up all the time I wasn't around."

Again Bolton paused for breath. Ki said, "I think I'm beginning to see what you're going to tell us, Mr. Bolton. You decided it was less harmful to both of you to let Ariane be what she was than to make her a prisoner."

"That's about the size of it." Bolton nodded. "Even if I didn't like it, leaving Ariane to do what she wanted sorta got her calmed down. Except I couldn't leave her around camp, the men got too riled up. So I got the idea of building her a little cabin away from camp, where she could do what she liked without keeping things stirred up the whole time. That's what I've been doing ever since."

Jessie spoke this time when Bolton paused. "I'm beginning to understand the situation now, Matt. You must've gone through some pretty bad hours."

"I'm not complaining, Miz Jessie. Like I said, it's not a real pretty story, but it's the truth, and I've learned not to let it bother me too much. I can sorta keep an eye on Ariane and see that she gets enough to eat and stays out of trouble."

"But you know what she's doing?" Ki asked.

"Sure, I know what she does, but now I'm real careful about the men I hire on, and I try to explain things to them. So far, it's worked out, even if I don't like the idea much."

"I'm not sure what I'd have done if I'd been in your place, Matt, but I can see your side of it," Jessie said. "And I guess I can see Ariane's as well. She can't help herself, and the only way you can help her is what you're doing now."

"That's the way I look at it," Bolton agreed. "But I try not to think about it too much, and it don't seem to bother Ariane."

"That's what I gathered after talking to her," Ki agreed. "She seemed very happy."

"Oh, she is," Bolton said. "So I can put up with it, even if it does hurt me sometimes."

"I'm not sure how I'd act, if I was in your place," Jessie said. "But from the way you've explained the situation, I can't see that you did anything other than what you found necessary."

"I've been sorta dreading having to tell you about her, but I knew I had to. I'm glad it's come out now."

"I think Jessie is, too," Ki put in. "And I know that I am. I thought I was beyond being surprised, but I was wrong."

"Well, it's a lot worse in winter, after the snow stops my logging work and I've got to take Ariane where there's strangers. But we move around a lot, and that's a help."

"Let's close the subject," Jessie suggested. "We've got trout waiting to be cooked, and I'll admit I'm getting hungry. We'll put off talking seriously until after dinner."

★

Chapter 10

"That was the best fish I've ever eaten," Jessie announced as she pushed her empty plate away. "And I include the meals I've enjoyed at places like Fisherman's Wharf and the Cliff House in San Francisco."

"There's only one way you'll get a better one," Bolton told her. "And that's to build a fire where you're starting to fish and cook whatever you catch as soon as you land it."

"I'll have to try that sometime," Jessie said. "I'll admit the idea appeals to me."

"We can try it up at the lake tomorrow, if you feel like it," Bolton offered. "Unless you and Ki have something more important to do."

"Unless Clem Harney gets back, we won't be doing much except looking around," Ki said. "Isn't that what you had in mind to do, Jessie?"

"Yes. We're not in a hurry, and there really isn't much we can do except look until Harney returns."

"I'd like to see him come back, too," Bolton put in. "I need to get back to my own work, and I still want to talk to him about moving up here as soon as we finish cutting what little timber there is on that stand I'm working."

"I can understand now why you're so anxious to get another stand of timber up here," Jessie told him. "Does Clem Harney know about your sister?"

"If he does, he hasn't told me so. But Clem sticks pretty

close to Sierra City. As far as I can see, he's a lot more interested in selling gold mining than he is in timber rights."

"Has he sold many mining claims?" Ki asked.

"I can't rightly say. He's real closemouthed about his business, and I'm not one to pry into his affairs. About all I ever heard him say was that he was going to push the claims that're nearest to Sierra City, and try to get them off his hands first."

"You wouldn't happen to know where the claims are that he's sold?" Jessie asked, keeping her voice carefully casual.

"Not right down to a tee, Miz Jessie. Like I told you before, what he's said a time or two gave me the idea that so far the only claims being worked are upslope, where the first prospectors got started before the big snow."

"That would be above the lake?" Ki asked.

"Mostly, I guess. At least, that's what I gathered," Bolton said.

Jessie turned to Ki. "Then suppose we get an early start tomorrow and go upslope."

"That suits me," Ki replied. "I've covered part of the ground down the slope, but I didn't see any signs of digging."

"You won't, either," Bolton put in. "Last week I put in two days walking the land below the town. I was trying to get an idea how much timber I could expect to cut if Clem does decide to sell me what I'm after. I didn't see signs of prospecting or mining anywhere down there."

"We'll look upslope tomorrow, then" Jessie told Ki. "We don't have much else to do until Harney gets back."

"There's always fish in the lake waiting to be caught," Bolton said, smiling.

"I'd enjoy catching another trout with you, Matt," Jessie told him. "But business comes first."

"When you've finished looking, then, Miz Jessie," Bolton told her. "But right now, I'd better be getting along.

You and Ki will want to turn in pretty soon if you're going to get an early start tomorrow."

"I'll be ready as soon as I buckle on my gunbelt," Jessie said as she and Ki got up from the table after a quick breakfast. "The sun's up now, so we won't be cold too long."

"Walking will warm us up," Ki replied. "And I'm as curious as you are about what we're going to find."

Skirting the side of the clearing away from the old hotel, Jessie and Ki walked unhurriedly up the slope in the direction of the little lake. They started up to the top of the ridge that ran above the meadow, walking in the shade, for the morning sun had not yet risen enough to send its rays over the crests of the high peaks that towered over them.

From the height of the ridge, Jessie could see for the first time the entire lake and the area around it. The meadow and the glistening lake looked smaller than they really were, and so did the houses of Sierra City. From above and at a distance, the signs of damage they'd suffered after being abandoned did not show. The straggling twin lines looked like any other small town that had not yet awakened for the day.

Beyond the houses the brush-dotted meadow gave way to the low undergrowth of bushes. The trail over which she and Ki had ridden into the dead town wound through the scrub like a carelessly tossed strand of brown rope. Past the point where the trail disappeared, the pines that remained after Matt Bolton's logging crews had done their work seemed thin in comparison with those that grew on the untouched slope that bordered the meadow.

Almost directly below, the surface of the lake was not as deep a blue in the still-forming day as it had appeared from below, and here and there the placid water was broken by the rings left by feeding trout. Now and again one of the fish leaped high enough to clear the water, and its silvery sides flashed for an instant before it fell back into the lake.

"This is a beautiful spot, Ki," Jessie said. "Since we've been up here, I'm not sure whether I'm glad or sorry that Alex decided not to build up here. Much as I love the Circle Star, this place has its own attractions."

"I don't know of any reason why you can't have both," Ki replied. "You already own the land, and those houses in Sierra City have plenty of well-seasoned lumber in them. It wouldn't be much of a job to build a permanent house here."

"I've had the same idea." Jessie nodded. "And now that we've smashed the cartel we don't have to live in a fortress any longer. I'll think about it some more. The idea certainly does appeal to me."

After they'd walked another quarter-mile the meadow was hidden by the towering pines, and the faint trail turned to go up the incline at a steeper angle. Still unaccustomed to the thin air of the high altitudes, both Jessie and Ki were panting a bit as they reached a spot where the trail curved from its uphill course and followed a stone-broken ledge around the mountainside. They had followed the faint trace for only a few dozen yards around the gently winding ledge when Jessie pointed ahead.

"Is that a cave?" she asked Ki. "Or has somebody started a mine shaft there?"

Ahead of them the steep side of the cliff that rose beside the path was broken by the black mouth of an opening that went into the mountainside.

"It doesn't look natural to me," Ki told her. "But we'll find out soon enough."

After they'd gotten closer it was easy to see that the arched black mouth of the opening was the work of man, not nature. There were clods of drying but still-fresh dirt strewn over the shelf along which the trail ran, and the symmetrical arc of the opening into the mountainside was obviously a miner's tunnel.

"We've found what we're looking for, Ki," Jessie said.

"I wonder if we can tell anything about it now that we've found it?"

"We'll know soon enough," Ki replied.

He kicked one of the big clods of dirt that lay on the narrow, almost invisible path they'd been following. The drying dirt crumbled readily, and as it flattened out it revealed a dozen or more pieces of whitish stone that had been buried inside the clod. Jessie picked up a small handful of the stones. She held them up into the light of the low-hanging rays of the early-morning sun that beamed through the close-spaced pines on the upslope, and exclaimed when she saw glints of yellow shining in the translucent stones.

Ki took one of the pieces of rock and held it up. When he looked closely at the stone, he could see the tiny pinpoint-sized flecks trapped in it glowing and reflecting the sunshine as it shone through the translucent rock.

"This is gold ore, Ki!" Jessie exclaimed. "There's no way of mistaking it for anything else!"

Ki nodded. "Those yellow spots are flecks of gold, all right," he agreed. "But it'd certainly be a lot of work to get them out of the rock."

"That's quartz rock, isn't it?" Jessie asked.

"I'm no mining expert, but I'm pretty sure it is," Ki replied.

He took another piece of the broken quartz and banged the two stones together with all his strength. The loose dirt clinging to them fell away and there was a brittle, cracking sound as the two pieces met, but neither broke.

"You were with Alex when he was developing the last of his Alaskan gold mines, Ki," Jessie went on. "Can you tell how much gold there is in these pieces of ore?"

"I'm afraid not, Jessie. That's an assayer's job, and it was quite a while ago when I went with Alex to Alaska. I know gold is trapped in the quartz, and the only way to get it out is to crush the rock to powder in a stamping mill.

Then it'd go in a sluice or trough of some kind to be washed. The gold would settle to the bottom and the quartz would be washed away."

"But that would take a lot of machinery and a tremendous amount of water," Jessie protested. "It'd be like the gold dredges that work in the streambeds. You'd have to wash tons and tons of crushed rock to get only a few ounces of gold."

"I'm afraid you're right, Jessie." Ki nodded. "There wouldn't be enough water in all of the Sierra Nevada range to process the amount of ore needed to make mining here profitable."

"So that's the swindle Harney's working on the people who buy his mining claims," Jessie exclaimed.

"It certainly looks that way," Ki agreed. "They'd be broke before they started if they had to spend ten dollars to get out two dollars' worth of gold."

"Harney must surely know that the claims he's selling are totally worthless."

"Of course he must," Ki said. "And I have a hunch that Alex lost interest in the land he bought up here because of the type of mining that would be necessary to get out the gold."

"Because there's so little gold in the quartz deposits." Jessie nodded.

"That, of course, and because of the way it'd have to be extracted. Taking out huge amounts of the quartz would tear up the mountains, for one thing."

"It'd spoil their peacefulness and beauty, I'm sure, and Alex was looking for a nice restful place," Jessie said.

"More than that," Ki went on. "If these gold deposits were ever mined, it would mean building a big stamping mill and an equally big smelter. That would really destroy the peace and quiet of the mountains."

"And now Harney's using Alex's good name to sell those claims!" Jessie said indignantly. "That's what makes me angrier than the swindle itself!"

"I'm positive we'd find several other claims just like this one if we kept looking." Ki frowned. "Do you think we've seen enough here to be sure of what's going on?"

"I certainly do!" Jessie replied. "But since I may have to take Harney into court to stop his cheating, I think I'd better set a trap for him, so that if I have to, I can testify myself that he tried to cheat me."

"That means you've definitely decided to let him sell you a claim, then?"

"That's the only way I can see to handle it, Ki. If you can think of a better way—"

"I can't at the moment," Ki told her. "Staying here another day or so while you let Harney persuade you to make an investment certainly can't do any harm. And who knows? We might turn up some more evidence that would help you if we stick around here a bit longer."

"Every bit of evidence we can get will help, of course," Jessie agreed. "And we certainly aren't pressed for time."

Jessie and Ki walked on along the quiet trail in the steadily brightening light of the new day. The mountains were beginning to waken now. Twice they came upon deer grazing beside the faintly marked trail—deer so unaccustomed to human contact that the animals did not bolt and run at once, but waited until the strolling pair was almost close enough to touch them before snorting in alarm, flagging their tails, and bolting off between the tall pines.

Small animals were out now, too. Chipmunks darted across the forest duff ahead of them, and birds chirped from the high branches of the pines. Once a badger waddled from the small scrub brush to cross the trail, and at one point they encountered a porcupine that did not move until Jessie and Ki were within a step or two, and then curled up into a ball to wait until they passed by.

During their short walk they also passed three more excavations a short distance off the trail, and each time they saw evidence of mining efforts they stopped to investigate the kind of gold ore the diggings had yielded. In every case the pieces of ore they found were exactly like those from the first of the abandoned claims, evidence that other gullible gold seekers lured by Harney's advertising had bought claims and then abandoned them after discovering that the ore they dug was valueless, regardless of the fact that it actually did contain some gold.

"Don't you think we've seen enough, Jessie?" Ki asked as they left the fourth dug-up spot on the mountains flanks.

"Yes. I'm sure any more of these claims we'd run into would be just the same," she said. "We might as well start back to Sierra City."

"Good. Because the morning's half gone by now, and my stomach keeps reminding me that we didn't have what you'd call a hearty breakfast." Ki smiled.

"We'll go back, then. I'm as hungry as you are, I'm sure."

They started to retrace their steps, the going much easier now that they were moving down the mountainside. The sun was high in the sky now, but the air was still crisply cool in the shade of the big pines that towered above the trail.

"Well, you certainly found what you were looking for," Ki remarked as they strolled leisurely along through the quiet pine forest. "Evidence that Harney's a swindler."

"And who knows how many more abandoned mines there are around here?" Jessie asked.

"Our friend Harney would know, I suppose," Ki replied. "But I'm not at all sure you could get him to tell you."

"No, but a judge will be able to make him talk when he questions him in a courtroom," Jessie said, traces of anger still in her voice. "And that's where I want to see Harney just as soon as I can manage to get him there."

"Do you think we've seen enough by now to go on with your plan?" Ki asked.

"Yes, I'm sure we have." Jessie nodded. "I had an idea we might find something like those claims, some real evidence that Harney really has sold some claims under fraudulent pretenses."

"Evidence enough to satisfy us," Ki cautioned. "But you'll need more than we've seen so far to make a case in court."

"Yes, I know. But if I buy a claim from Harney and find it has gold on it that can't be sold, I can get on the witness stand myself and testify how I was cheated."

"That ought to clinch a case against Harney, but I'm not sure how a judge might take your testimony, Jessie."

"How do you mean?"

"You want to stop Harney's swindle, but you also want to get his agreement with Alex declared invalid," Ki explained. "That would make you a prejudiced witness."

"I'm sure that Frank Allison's a good enough lawyer to get around that," Jessie said confidently. "But I'll talk to him about that point before I do anything, of course."

By this time they'd reached the portion of the trail from which the lake was visible. Its character had changed more than that of the land around it. The breeze had died as the sun climbed higher, and the water was no longer still, nor was it a deep, mysterious blue. Now its shade matched the lighter hue of the sky, and the water's surface was rippled with many rings where feeding trout had broken the water when they fed.

Before the lake was shielded from sight by the trees again, a dark dot suddenly broke the rippled surface near the center and started purposefully toward shore, leaving a widening V behind it. Jessie stopped and Ki stopped with her, watching the swimming creature as it moved to shore and emerged from the water, an elongated animal with stubby legs and a long tail.

"It's an otter!" Jessie exclaimed as the animal scurried away from the lakeshore and disappeared into the trees. "I've seen them before, in the streams up in Oregon and Washington."

115

"I imagine you'd see all sorts of wildlife if you stayed around here a little while," Ki remarked. "But right now I'm only interested in animals that I can eat."

"We'll hurry on down the rest of the way, then," Jessie said. "I suddenly seem to be as hungry as you are. It must be this crisp mountain air."

They moved on, the trail slanting more sharply downward now, and in a few moments they were at the edge of the mountain meadow where Sierra City stood. The meadow had been hidden from the trail by the towering pines, and when Jessie looked across it toward Sierra City, she turned to Ki and pointed toward it.

"Matt must have seen those trout jumping, too," Jessie said. "Here he comes with his fishing pole."

"Are you going to go with him?" Ki asked. "I remember that he invited you yesterday evening."

"I don't know whether I'd rather catch another trout or go on to Sierra City and get something to eat," Jessie said.

Bolton was within hailing distance of them now. He waved and called, "How do you feel about fishing today, Miz Jessie? When I looked out at the lake a while ago and saw those rises, I just couldn't stay away. Are you too tired to join me?"

Jessie hesitated for only a moment, then the memory of her earlier catch flashed into her mind. She said, "Not a bit, Matt, if you're sure you want an amateur along."

"There's only one way for an amateur to get to be a fisherman," Bolton told her. "That's by fishing."

"I'll go with you, then," she said. Turning to Ki, she went on, "Matt's right, you know. And I did enjoy catching that trout yesterday."

"Good luck, then." Ki nodded. "I'll look for you when you get back."

★

Chapter 11

"We'd better go on around to the inlet," Matt Bolton told Jessie as they left Ki and walked on along the path through the meadow. "I've fished this lake enough to find out that the trout seem to gather up there at this time of day."

"How do you learn where the fish are in a lake?" Jessie asked. "Doesn't it take a lot of time?"

"Oh, I don't know, Miz Jessie. I guess I just figure out after a while what the fish will do. Don't ask me how."

"I'll make a deal with you," Jessie offered. "I won't ask you how if you'll stop calling me 'miss.' It makes me feel like we're still strangers."

"Calling ladies 'miss' is something my mother taught me," Bolton told her. "Down south where she came from, it's the way men talk. But Jessie it'll be from now on, if that suits you best."

"It does," Jessie said. She looked ahead and through the close-standing bushes that grew profusely between the path and the water's edge saw the sun dancing from the rippling water of the creek that fed the lake. She asked Bolton, "Is this where we're heading for?"

"It's as good a place as any," he replied. "All we're looking for is a place where we can cast a fly out into the current so it'll be carried out to where the trout are feeding."

Holding the long rod above his head, Bolton pushed

through the thick bushes ahead of Jessie, opening a path for her. As they reached the water's edge, a muted splash sounded a dozen feet from the inlet, and Bolton pointed to the bubbles that floated on the disturbed water.

"That was a big trout," he told her. "The big ones don't jump, they just come up and gulp down what they want. See if you can get him to take a fly."

"No, you cast first," Jessie urged. "Show me what to do."

"That's something else my mother taught me, Jessie," he replied. "It's always ladies first." He held out the rod. "Go on and catch that fellow. Just cast up where the creek runs in, and let the current pull your fly under and take it down to the lake. Leave your line loose so the current can work the fly naturally."

Seeing that protest would do no good, Jessie took the rod and, after two failures to make a cast, finally placed the fly where Bolton had told her to. She watched the tiny blob of feathers sink, and felt the line tighten as the current took it.

"What do I do when—" she began, turning to Bolton, but before she could finish her question the line tightened and the rod began bending. Surprised by the trout's quick response, her hand froze on the reel's handle.

"Let him run!" Bolton exclaimed.

He spoke too late. The rod reached the limit of its arc, then the tip flipped up as the delicate, invisible leader snapped and the line went limp.

"He broke the line!" Jessie exclaimed. "I didn't let go of the reel quick enough!"

"Don't worry. There's plenty more out there," Bolton told her. "Just reel the line in and I'll put on another fly."

Jessie reeled in until the dangling leader emerged from the water. She raised the tip of the rod and swung the thin, almost invisible strand of gut toward her until she could grasp it. Bolton had taken out a small tin box and was picking out a fresh fly.

He stepped up in front of Jessie and took the tip of the broken leader, threaded it into the eye of the hook, and started to form a knot, but his fingers fumbled when he handled the almost-invisible leader. While he was trying to form the knot a gust of wind pulled the line from his hands.

Shaking his head, he said, "This is the wrong place for me to be. I'm used to holding the rod and tying knots while I'm looking down at them. This way, I feel like I'm working backward."

"Step around behind me, then," Jessie suggested. "You can look over my shoulder while you tie the knot."

"That'll be better," he said. Moving behind her, he stepped up and slid his hands under Jessie's arms, reaching for the whipping end of the leader that was now swaying in front of him.

Again the wind pulled the almost-invisible gut out of his reach. Bolton lunged to catch it, managed to get it into his hand, and brought his other arm up around Jessie to get a firmer grip on the leader. His move put them into an embrace, and Jessie turned her head to look at him.

Their heads were only an inch or two apart, their bodies pressing together, with Bolton's arm closed around Jessie's burgeoning breasts, holding her to him. For a moment their eyes met, then Bolton leaned forward and closed the small gap between them as he sought her lips with his.

Although Bolton's embrace had been totally unexpected, it was not unwelcome to Jessie, for as Bolton's lips met hers she realized that almost since their first meeting she'd been drawn to the genial, unassuming logger. She turned her body toward him, and as her breasts brushed against his muscular chest she felt their tips beginning to bud.

Bolton's lips on hers were more insistent now. He was moving them as though he was trying to talk, but when Jessie opened her lips his tongue quickly slipped between them, and she met it with hers. She started to raise her hands to clasp Bolton around the neck, and realized belatedly that she was still holding the fishing rod. She tried to push it aside, but Bolton's arms were grasping her to him, and she could not let the long bamboo rod fall. Cupping his chin in her free hand, she broke their kiss gently.

"This fishing pole's coming between us," she said. "If you'll let go of me for a minute, I'll get rid of it."

For a moment she thought he was going to ignore her suggestion, then he slowly lowered one arm and let her push the rod away. Before it had fallen to the ground, Bolton's arms were grasping her firmly again, his lips working insistently against hers, and now Jessie could respond freely. Her tongue darted out to meet his, and they stood in their close embrace until lack of breath forced them to separate.

"I—I didn't really mean to grab you," Bolton began as he gasped for breath. "But ever since I saw you the first time I've wanted to reach out and pull you into my arms."

"I'm glad you did," Jessie told him in a half-whisper. "I like the feel of your arms around me."

"You don't think—" he began, but Jessie freed one arm in a flash of motion and pressed his lips closed with her finger.

"This isn't a time to think," she said. "It's a time to do what our nature tells us to."

"You really mean that?"

"Of course I do. If I hadn't meant it, I'd have kept quiet and pushed you away."

"Then let's not stay out here in the open any longer. If we get into the brush, nobody will be able to see us."

A scant half-dozen steps separated them from the shielding bushes, and they hurried hand in hand into the shelter the thick growth provided. A grassed-over spot a few steps deeper into the concealing bushes caught Jessie's eye at once. She stopped, and Bolton pulled her to him again. In close embrace they sank to the ground, the soft cushion of high, thick grass cushioning them.

Bolton's hands were at the throat of Jessie's blouse in an

120

instant, fumbling at its buttons. Jessie helped him to shrug the blouse free of her shoulders and he pulled it down, baring her bulging breasts with their budded pink tips. He bent to caress the soft white globes with his lips.

As Bolton leaned over Jessie and began kissing her upthrust breasts and caressing their pebbled rosettes with his lips and tongue, she slipped a hand down to his crotch. Through the coarse cloth of his logger's jeans, she felt the generous bulge of his erection. For a moment she was content to stroke the bulge, then the warm thrusting of Bolton's tongue filling her willing mouth brought a sudden impatience, and Jessie began unbuttoning his jeans.

She was responding fully by now to the caresses and kisses that Bolton's lips were tracing from her lips to the column of her throat and down to her budded breasts. As his tongue again touched the pink protruding tips of her quivering globes Jessie finally liberated him, and closed her hand around his burgeoning shaft. Bolton's muscles tightened when he felt her warm hand grasping him and he moved instinctively, lifting his hips in response to the pressure of Jessie's soft, warm hand.

Jessie was ready for him now. She continued her caresses with one soft hand while she reached to lift her skirt and slip down her pantalettes, then tugged at him urgently as she parted her thighs.

Bolton needed no urging beyond the pressure of Jessie's fingers. He rose above her and, as she guided him with gentle but urgent touches, he sank between her welcoming silken thighs until he was filling her completely.

Neither of them moved for a moment; they were content to lie quietly and enjoy their joining. Then Bolton started stroking. For several minutes he moved gently and slowly, then as Jessie responded by meeting his thrusts he came to sudden life. The tempo of his deep lunges quickened even more, until Jessie gasped with increasing pleasure as she felt herself mounting to a climax, and rocked her hips to match his plunges.

She quickly matched the rhythm he was setting, her hips threshing furiously as the sensations swept her quivering body. When she felt Bolton starting to tremble with the beginning of his spasm, she was on the verge of her own, gasping as her body quivered with readiness. He moaned loudly and sank into her with a final deep thrust, and Jessie abandoned herself to the surges that shook her as she reached her peak. She cried out with her fulfillment while Bolton lurched with a last gasping spasm, then they both subsided and lay limp and spent, their passion drained.

Minutes passed before Jessie was again aware of the soft susurrus of the lake's tiny wavelets breaking against the shore. She stirred and Bolton left her, stretching out on the thick grass beside her.

"I honestly didn't plan to—" he began.

Jessie interrupted. "Neither did I. But we both had the same idea at the same time. We don't have anything to regret."

"You really mean that, don't you, Jessie?" he asked, propping himself up on an elbow now to look down on her.

"Of course I do. Why would I say something I don't mean?"

"Because some women do. But you're different. Maybe that's why I felt attracted to you the first time I saw you."

"If you did, you didn't show it."

"How could I? That wasn't the time or place. Except for our fishing trip yesterday, this was the first chance we've had to be alone together. But I hope it won't be the last."

"We'll make chances to be alone if we want them," Jessie told him.

They lay in silence for a few moments, then Bolton lifted himself on an elbow and looked down at Jessie, a small frown wrinkling his forehead.

"Who are you really?" he asked. "I'm sure that Jessie's not your full name. Can't you tell me what your last name is?"

"Please don't ask me any questions, Matt," Jessie said.

"I have plenty of good reasons for asking you. If it'll ease your mind, I'm not running or hiding from anybody—a jealous husband, for instance—and I'm not breaking any laws. If things work out, I'll tell you the whole story later."

"What things—?" Bolton began, then realized by questioning her he was doing what she'd asked him not to. He fell silent for a moment, then went on, "All right. I won't pry into your private life any more. But you'll tell me before you leave, won't you?"

"Yes. I promise you I will, Matt."

Bolton looked at her in silence for another moment, then the puzzled frown on his face faded and was replaced with a smile. He said, "The trout are waiting for us out in the lake, but I've suddenly lost interest in them. Don't you think there are better things for us to do than fishing?"

"I'm sure there must be," Jessie said, extending her arms to him. "And if you'll start by kissing me again, I think we can find out very soon exactly what they are."

"You fished much longer than I expected you to," Ki said as Jessie entered the house. "It's getting so dark that I was thinking of lighting the lamp. But where are your fish?"

"I'm afraid I didn't bring any trout home today," Jessie replied. Then, staying with the literal truth, she went on, "The only trout that really struck hard broke my fly off."

"And Matt? He didn't do any better?"

"I'm afraid not."

"I'll fix us some supper, then," Ki said. "But before I start, I have some news. And I think perhaps our waiting for Clem Harney is finished."

"You mean he's gotten back from wherever he was?"

"About a half-hour ago a man rode onto the meadow and went directly to the old hotel," Ki said. "Of course, I can't be sure it was Harney, because I don't know what he looks like. But he acted as though he belongs here, so I'm guessing that's who he is."

"That's really good news, Ki," Jessie said. "I'm anxious

to hear what kind of story he has to tell."

"And even more important, to see what he has to sell," Ki added. "And how he goes about explaining it."

"Oh, he'll have some plausible story," Jessie said. "You can be sure of that. After all the confidence men who've tried to trick me into one scheme or another since Alex died, I'm sure I can recognize the breed when I run into another one."

"I wouldn't doubt that for a minute," Ki assured her. "Now, do you want to go up to the old hotel and see what Mr. Clem Harney is like?"

Jessie thought for a moment, then shook her head. "No, I think I'll let Mr. Harney come down here and see us."

"In other words, you don't want to appear too anxious." Ki nodded. "If that's the case, then, I'll get busy and fix our supper. Perhaps we can finish eating before Harney shows up."

They had finished eating supper and Ki had just put away the dishes after washing and drying them when a rapping on the door broke the companionable silence which Jessie and Ki had long ago learned to share when one of them was busy.

Under her breath, Jessie said, "That will probably be our friend Harney. Would you mind answering the door, Ki, as long as you're on your feet?"

Ki opened the door. The light from the lamp on the table in the center of the room showed a tall, sinewy man standing in the doorway. He wore no hat, and the lamplight glistened on his balding head. A thin line of bushy salt-and-pepper sideburns framed his saturnine face, which was marked by heavy eyebrows, small, cold ice-blue eyes, a craggy aquiline nose, thin lips, and a narrow, jutting jaw.

For a moment the man swept Ki with a quick flick of his eyes. Then he said, "You'd answer to the name of Ki, I imagine, from what Matt Bolton said, and the lady sitting over there must be Miss Jessie."

"That's right." Ki nodded.

"And I'm sure you know who I am," the newcomer went on, his eyes moving back and forth from Ki to Jessie. "Clem Harney. I'm sorry you had to wait for me to get back to Sierra City, but I had to attend to some urgent business in San Francisco. I have very extensive holdings there, you understand."

"I'm sure you're busy, Mr. Harney," Jessie said. "We haven't minded the wait a bit. Your friend Mr. Bolton was kind enough to look after us. But do come in."

"Good, good." Harney stepped inside and placed his hat on the table. "I suppose you've come to find out about the ads I've been running in the newspapers?"

"That's what we have in mind," Jessie replied.

"If you want to get rich, you've really come to the right place," Harney went on.

"Do sit down and tell us about the gold-mining claims, Mr. Harney," Jessie said. "Your advertisements made them sound very, very attractive."

Harney settled into the chair nearest him. "Well, I'm glad you think so, ma'am. There's gold all around us, plenty of it. But it's a bit late for me to tell you about everything tonight, so tomorrow morning it'll be my pleasure to do that. Or we could talk about it this evening, if you're not too tired."

"Tomorrow would be better," Jessie replied. "I'm not used to the altitude yet, and I've done a lot of walking since we got here. I'm sure Ki is as tired as I am."

"Then I won't keep you from retiring," Harney said, standing up. "I'll bid you good evening now, and we'll start bright and early in the morning. I'm sure that by this time tomorrow evening you'll be putting your feet on the road that will make you very rich indeed."

★

Chapter 12

"Well, what do you think, Jessie?" Ki asked as the sound of Clem Harney's retreating footsteps faded and died away.

"I think we've just been visited by a man who makes his money by cheating unsuspecting people out of theirs," Jessie replied. "All the time he was here he tried to give us the impression that he's doing us a favor, but his eyes were flicking around, sizing us up, like he was trying to figure how much money we might have."

"He certainly has all the earmarks of a confidence man," Ki agreed. "Even though I have to admit he's got a good spiel."

"A very good one, unless you've run into it before," Jessie said. "Still, I don't think I'd be inclined to trust our Mr. Harney to tell me the truth if I asked him the time of day."

"I think you're going to be more than he can handle, Jessie."

"We'll give him all the rope he'll take, and let him trip himself up," Jessie went on thoughtfully. "Then we'll turn him over to the authorities. They can handle the rest of it."

"Are you sure you won't catch Matt Bolton with the same rope?" Ki asked. "He and Harney seem to be pretty good friends. They might be working in cahoots."

"I doubt it," Jessie replied. "I'm sure Matt's only interest is what he told me. He's trying to lease the logging and timber rights on this land Harney pretends to control, so he can't know that those rights aren't really Harney's to lease."

"Then you don't think he sees through Harney?"

Jessie shook her head. "Matt's not a devious man, Ki. All he's interested in is cutting timber. And fishing, of course."

"He won't get in our way, will he?"

"I don't see how he could," Jessie said. "Anyhow, he'll probably leave tomorrow to go back to his timber lease. I imagine he'll stop on the way long enough to say good-bye."

"I think I'll go to bed, then." Ki yawned. "This cool mountain air makes me sleepy."

"It does me, too," Jessie said. "And there's nothing more that we can do tonight. But tomorrow's likely to be a very busy day."

"I guess our friend Matt Bolton decided not to stop by before starting back to his logging camp after all," Ki remarked as he and Jessie sat at breakfast the following morning.

"Matt probably started out early," Jessie said. "He told me yesterday that he was anxious to get back to work. I imagine he passed here before we got up, and didn't want to disturb us. If he's still here, I'll see him when I go down to the old hotel to talk to Harney."

"It'll be interesting to see what Harney comes up with next," Ki said. "And even more interesting when he finds out who you are."

"From the way he's started, that'll be very soon," Jessie told him. "And as soon as I get the evidence that he's using Alex's good name in a swindling scheme, I don't intend to waste any time in filing a complaint. At least we can protect some innocent people from throwing away their life's savings."

"You seem to have your plans pretty well made," Ki

128

commented, then asked, "You're sure it would be better for you to talk to Harney alone?"

"Very sure, Ki," Jessie replied as she stood up. "He'll talk more freely if there's nobody with me to testify against him, and one of the things I'm counting on is letting his own words prove he's guilty when we get him to court. This morning I'm going to go back to being a wooly sheep waiting to be fleeced, and let Harney show his hand."

"Ah, good morning, Miss Jessie!" Clem Harney said as he opened the door of the old hotel building. "Bright and early, I see, just as we said last night. But come in, and we'll have our little visit. I'm sure you'll feel better when I've answered those questions you asked me."

"Are we the only ones here?" Jessie asked as she entered the big main room and settled down in the chair Harney hurried to bring her. "I thought Mr. Bolton was staying with you."

"He was, but he left very early. He was anxious to get back to his own business. I'm sure he must have mentioned to you that he's a lumberman. He has a crew of men in a logging camp lower down the mountain."

"Yes, he did say something about that when he introduced himself the day we got here," Jessie replied.

"I must apologize again for not being here to greet you, but I'm sure you understand why."

"Oh, of course. A man as busy as you seem to be must have to use every minute of his time, I imagine," Jessie said guilelessly. "But there are one or two things I'm curious about, Mr. Harney."

"I'll be glad to answer your questions. Just explain what's bothering you."

"It's been quite a while since I saw your first newspaper advertisement about this place, but I don't see any signs of other people around here," Jessie said. "Yet Mr. Bolton told me people have bought claims. Where are all the buyers?"

"All the buyers so far have needed time to settle their affairs wherever they've been living, so none of them have moved up here yet," Harney replied smoothly.

"Then Ki and I are the only ones staying here?"

"Right now you are. But I ran another advertisement in the Sunday papers last week, so I imagine there'll be some more folks who'll show up after a day or two. Now, what else is it that bothers you?"

"Are you sure there's lots of gold up here?" she went on.

"Don't worry about that, either," Harney replied instantly, in a glib fashion that told Jessie her question was a common one and Harney's answer was one frequently used. "It's all around us, plenty of it."

Concerned that Bolton might have mentioned the exploration that she and Ki had made of the abandoned claims, Jessie said, "I asked Mr. Bolton about the mining claims that people have bought earlier, and went up with Ki to look at some that he told us were higher up on the mountain, but we didn't find anybody. Just some holes that looked like somebody had started and then stopped digging."

"Bolton doesn't understand about mining, I'm afraid," Harney said quickly. "He's a lumberman, of course, so he's really just used to cutting trees."

"But he said—"

"Never mind what he said!" Harney broke in, his voice edgy. He recovered his poise quickly and went on, "Now, let me ask you, how much do you know about gold mining and ore deposits?"

"Well—" Jessie hesitated for a moment. "I really don't know much, except that you have to dig up the gold ore and have it—melted, isn't that it?"

"Not melted, Miss Jessie—smelted. That's to get the dirt and rock out. What a smelter really does is just clean the gold ore."

"I think I understand that," Jessie said.

"Well, then, you might be interested to know that I intend to build a smelter close by to handle the ore from the mining claims people invest in. Of course, the men working in the smelter and the mines will have to live here in Sierra City. You can imagine how the town will grow."

"Oh, my, yes!" Jessie said, nodding. "It looks like you really do have good prospects of bringing it back to life."

"I'm confident it will grow!" Harney said enthusiastically. "Give me a year, and Sierra City will be even more thriving than it ever was before!"

"I suppose some stores will open up again when the people who've bought places from you start moving in," Jessie said thoughtfully.

"Oh, yes, indeed. You can count on that happening. Sierra City's going to be a live town again before too long, perhaps even a very big town, and the ones who're here first will be in a situation to make a lot of money out of whatever they invest in the place right now."

"Yes, I can see how that would be the case," Jessie replied. She didn't mention that Alex had been responsible for starting a half-dozen new communities in the West and that she herself had been instrumental in bringing two or three new towns to life in connection with her inheritance from him.

"It's something to think about," Harney went on. "Of course, I don't know what your situation is, ma'am, but if you decide against gold mining there's a big opportunity here for you to make an investment in commercial property."

"I can see that, now that you've mentioned it," Jessie said. "It would be nice to see these houses all lighted up at night. I—well, I feel a little uncomfortable here now. It's so dark and quiet when the sun goes down."

"Mentioning lights reminds me of something else you might be considering, Miss Jessie," Harney said. "As Sierra City grows bigger there'll be a demand for piped-in gas to provide light."

"I suppose that's true." Jessie nodded. "I know a lot of cities have gaslight now, but isn't this place a little bit out of the way for a convenience like that?"

"Not at all! We'll need a big plant to furnish gas for our smelter, anyway."

"Isn't that going to cost a lot of money?"

"Certainly. As well-off as I am, I couldn't finance both the smelter and the gasworks myself, so I'm forming two stock companies, one to build the smelter, the other to build the gas-generating plant. I want the gasworks to be big enough to provide piped-in gas for the houses and stores in Sierra City."

"I'm very impressed, Mr. Harney. That certainly shows a lot of forethought."

"Just good, practical business judgment, that's all. The point that I'm making is that a small investment now in a gas generator and some pipe would certainly bring rich dividends in the future."

"What would you call a small investment?"

"Oh, perhaps five thousand dollars in each plant," Harney said casually. "But what I'm trying to tell you is that if you decide against trying your hand at gold mining, some stock in the smelter and the Sierra City Gas Company will certainly grow in value. The stock alone could make you rich."

"That is a thought," Jessie said. "But I'd think you'd want to reserve an improvement of that kind for yourself."

"Why, I'm not a greedy man, Miss Jessie," Harney protested. "And of course, my main interest is in the land itself. I want to see the town grow. But I'd happily share my good fortune with you and others who are wise enough to invest now."

"Well, that does you a great deal of credit," Jessie told him, giving Harney plenty of rope, as she'd told Ki. "We'll have to discuss that, too, after I've had a chance to look around a little bit more. I really came up here because of the gold claims, of course, and I want to look at them first."

"And I want you to see them. But there's one more thing I'd better mention." Harney hitched his chair closer to Jessie's, bent forward, and dropped his voice to a whisper as he went on, "Can I trust you to keep something completely confidential?"

"Well, of course!" Jessie replied, her voice feigning indignation. "I've had a bit of business experience myself, you know, and I understand how important some things are."

"Of course you do." Harney nodded. "As I told you, Matt Bolton doesn't know much about mining—or much about my plans for Sierra City."

"Did we go to the wrong places, then?"

"I'll tell you the answer to that in just a moment." Harney looked around the room as though he were afraid there might be someone else present, then went on, "You've heard that gold mining is a very competitive business, I'm sure."

"Yes, that's why I wondered about your advertising these claims up here for sale."

"A smokescreen, Miss Jessie. Advertisements like that always bring out a lot of people who don't have the financial stability that I'm sure you enjoy. Now, the gold in the claims you visited is what we call quartziferous, which means the metal is in quartz crystals that have to be crushed and smelted. Do you follow me?"

"I'm afraid I don't."

"Quartziferous gold is the richest kind," Harney continued in the same low whisper. "Placer gold is the easiest to get at."

"Isn't placer gold the kind they pan for in the foothills?" Jessie asked.

"Exactly. But not very many people realize the special value of quartziferous gold. I want to keep the most desirable claims for myself and a small, select group of shrewd investors. I think you qualify for that select group."

"My goodness!" Jessie protested. "I don't see how you can say that, Mr. Harney! You only met me yesterday!"

"I'm relying on my intuition. I'm a very shrewd judge of character," he replied. "Even though we've just met, I've formed an excellent opinion of you, and my opinions are seldom wrong. Now, I'll tell you what I intend to do. I'm going to let you in on my secret plans. Will you swear to keep them a close secret?"

"Of course I will!"

"Good. Buy all the quartziferous claims you can afford. They will produce three to four times as much gold as placer claims. They'll make you rich beyond your wildest dreams. And I'll also let you in on the group of inside investors in the smelter and gas company. The stock in them will double your returns in a very short time."

"I—I hardly know what to say," Jessie told Harney.

"Don't say anything until you've looked around, just as you planned to do when you came up here. Then we'll sit down and talk, and you can decide how much you're able to invest. Now, do you think I could offer you anything fairer than that?"

"Why—why no, I don't suppose so," Jessie stammered, feigning total astonishment. "But how much would you expect me to invest?"

"As much as you can afford," Harney said. "Could you put in—oh, let's say fifty thousand dollars, to become a multimillionaire?"

"Maybe not quite that much," Jessie replied after a moment of silence. "Twenty thousand, perhaps as much as thirty."

"That's a relatively small amount." Harvey frowned. "But in your case, I'll make an exception and accept it."

"I didn't bring the money with me," Jessie said.

"That's wise." Harney nodded. "I imagine it's in a bank, isn't it?"

"Yes. But if you'll take a check—"

"A check will be quite satisfactory," he said. "But I don't want you to put up a dime until you've looked at the rest of the claims."

"Of course," she agreed. "But you'll have to tell me how to find them."

"Straight up the mountainside," Harney answered. "It's not much of a climb, if that bothers you. Just follow the trail to where you must've turned off the other day, and keep going up. You won't have any trouble finding the claims, there'll be fresh dirt all around them."

"It isn't a hard trail to follow, I hope?"

"Not a bit hard. I'd go with you myself, but I have a few pieces of important unfinished business to attend to."

"I don't imagine Ki and I will have any trouble," Jessie told him. "And then you and I can talk again when we get back."

"We most certainly can!" Harney assured her. "Whenever it's convenient, after you get back."

"Ki and I will start right away, then," she said.

"Harney's a crook, all right," Jessie told Ki a few minutes later, when she returned to the cabin where they were staying. "It's a waste of talent, in a way. He could make a fortune writing fairy tales. You can't guess what he tried to sell me as an alternative to a gold claim."

"I won't even try to guess," Ki replied. "For all I know, it might've been the shirt off his back."

"Nothing quite as useful, Ki." Jessie smiled. "He suggested that I might make a lot of money investing in an imaginary smelter and an equally imaginary gas-generating plant for Sierra City."

"But so far he's the only one who lives here!"

"That didn't slow him down any. He moved from a gold-mine claim to the gasworks without blinking an eyelid."

"And you encouraged him, of course?"

"I barely needed to. One minute he was telling me how tremendously rich one of his gold claims would make me, and the next thing I knew he was telling me how I could get even richer by investing in the gas-generating plant he plans to build to pipe gas for lighting the houses up here."

"You'd hardly get rich that way, Jessie, with nobody to buy the gas even if it was available," Ki observed.

"Oh, he sketched a really prosperous future for Sierra City when all the gold miners and smelter operators and shopkeepers move here. But that's the point I'm making," Jessie went on. "I've had enough business experience to know what the pitfalls are. I'm not sure others would, and they're the ones who're victimized by confidence men like Harney."

"Did he mention Alex at all?"

"No. Not this time. He didn't mention him last night either, but I'm sure he will when we talk more about the most preposterous offer he made. I haven't even gotten around to telling you about that one yet."

"Well, don't keep me waiting," Ki said.

"Did you know those abandoned quartziferous claims we looked at yesterday are better than placer claims, Ki?"

For a moment Ki stared incredulously, then he asked, "Did Harney actually tell you that, Jessie, or is this a joke?"

"I felt like asking Harney that," Jessie replied. "But do you know, Ki, he spun me a yarn that almost seemed plausible, even if I did know that placer mining is the cheapest way to get gold out of the ground."

"Yes." Ki nodded. "I remember when we were battling the gold dredges in the valley. They were operating profitably when they got a half-ounce of gold out of every ton of river-bottom mud they put through their sluices."

"Harney had the nerve to tell me that quartziferous ore is the most valuable. I almost said something then, but I stopped just in time. He's very good at what he does, though."

"That alone makes him dangerous enough to stop."

"What I want to do is keep him from continuing to use Alex's name in his advertising to lend credence to his crooked schemes."

"I suppose you have a plan?"

"Part of one. We'll have to go look at the claims Harney told me about first, because I'm sure he'll be watching us pretty closely. We can talk about plans on the way."

★

Chapter 13

As they walked toward the old hotel, Jessie said to Ki, "I'll agree to buy a claim from Harney, and you can be there as a witness."

"We didn't bring all that much cash with us," Ki reminded her. "And you can't give him a check signed Jessie Starbuck."

"I've thought of a way around that, Ki. I'm counting on Harney preferring cash to a check, so I'll give him a couple of hundred dollars out of our traveling cash as earnest money and promise to meet him in San Francisco in a few days to make the full payment. And I'll tell him it will be in cash, too," Jessie said. "I'm sure he'll agree to that, because for one thing cash can't be traced, but a check can."

"Yes, I'm sure Harney will think of that, too," Ki told her. "It looks to me like you're setting a pretty good trap."

"Of course, I'm counting on Harney overlooking something," Jessie went on.

"What's that?"

"He'll have to give me a receipt," Jessie answered. "I'm counting on him being so greedy that he'll overlook the fact that his receipt is just as good as a check for evidence that he tried to swindle me."

Ki nodded and said, "I'm following you, Jessie. As soon as you get the receipt we'll take it to the sheriff in

Truckee, and swear out an arrest warrant."

"Exactly," she replied. "The sheriff and the court can do the rest."

"That should stop him," Ki agreed. "And I'm sure you've already planned to get back that agreement Alex made with Harney for mineral rights to this land."

"Why, certainly. That's the main reason I'm taking all this time and trouble. I don't like it when swindlers rob people by using the reputation for fair dealing that Alex earned."

They reached the old hotel building. A light gleamed through the lower-floor windows, and when Jessie rapped on the door Harney opened it so quickly she was sure he'd been waiting for her to show up.

"Good morning, Miss Jessie." He smiled. "You must be on your way up the mountain to look at those gold claims I told you about last night."

"We are," Jessie said. "But I wanted to stop on the way and tell you what I think I'll do about the investments you explained to me last night."

"I hope you've had time to consider them carefully," Harney told her.

"Oh, I certainly have," Jessie replied.

"Then suppose you and Ki come in and sit down while we talk. It's still nippy out here, and we might as well be comfortable."

"I've thought a great deal about the amount of money I can afford to invest," Jessie said to Harney as they settled into chairs in the cavernous room that had been the hotel's lobby. "You explained things to me so clearly last night that I want to put all the money I can afford into your development up here."

"Now, that's a very wise decision." Harney nodded. "I'm glad my explanations helped you."

"Oh, they did," Jessie said. "Now, I told you yesterday that the most I could invest was thirty thousand dollars, but after I thought about things, I've decided to mortgage my house. I'm sure I can raise about fifteen thousand dollars that way."

"Which would bring your investment up to forty-five thousand," Harney said. "That's very shrewd. You'll get enough income from your stock to pay the mortgage off very fast."

"That's what I thought, after what you told me. But taking out a mortgage worries me a little bit," Jessie went on, "since I'll be putting almost every penny I've got into the stock as well. Are you absolutely sure your development of Sierra City and the gold mines up here will be profitable, Mr. Harney?"

"Can you name a better investment than solid gold?" Harney countered. "That's why people call something 'as good as gold'! If you follow my advice you'll be a very rich lady in just a short time."

"Well, I'm glad to hear you say that," Jessie said. "Now, I didn't bring a great deal of money with me, but if you'll accept a few hundred dollars as a—well, I guess you'd call it a sort of option. Isn't that the word?"

"It's the exact word, Miss Jessie," Harney replied. "Go on and explain what you have in mind."

"I thought that if you'll let me give you a few hundred dollars as an option, I can go down to the bank in Truckee and have them send a telegram to transfer my money from the bank in San Francisco right away. Then, after I get back home, I can arrange the mortgage and send you the rest of the money."

"Why, that will be perfectly satisfactory!" Harney said, almost visibly trying to restrain the appearance of being anxious to get his hands on Jessie's cash.

"But first I'm going up with Ki to look at those gold claims you told me about," Jessie said quickly. "I intend to make sure there's as much gold in them as you say."

"You'll find that there is," Harney assured her.

"Then if you'll make out an agreement while Ki and I go up and look at the claims, we'll finish everything else

141

when I get back, and then I'll start for home," Jessie said, standing up.

"As I told you yesterday, you'll find the claims are very rich," Harney said as he followed Jessie's example and got to his feet. "Now, just go straight on up the mountain instead of turning off on that tail you took the other day. And take your time looking around. I'll be ready when you get back."

After they'd left Sierra City and were halfway across the meadow on the trail that led up the mountain slopes, Ki turned to Jessie.

"You're a better confidence man than Harney is," he said with a smile. "Why, you even had me feeling sorry for you when you gave him that story about sinking your last pennies into his cheating scheme."

"I've learned a lot from the dozens of confidence men who've tried to swindle me before he came along," Jessie told him. "You've seen how they lead their victims on with a story that doesn't give them time to think rationally because they're dazzled by the idea of all the quick money they expect to make instead of worrying about how much they stand to lose."

"Well, you certainly did an expert job of table-turning," Ki went on. "And you even gave Harney something to keep him busy while we're gone, so he won't have time to think about what you said and find holes in your yarn."

"I'm hoping we can find holes in Harney's yarn to me when we get to those claims he says are up there," Jessie said as they reached the foot of the slope and started up the mountain's flank. "I don't think I'm suspicious by nature, Ki, but when someone's working a scheme like Harney's, I distrust just about everything he recommends."

"We'll know soon enough," Ki told her. "But starting out by being suspicious is a pretty good way to keep from being fooled."

They walked on up the slope, which grew steadily

142

steeper as they got higher up on the mountain's flank. Here the big pines appeared to be slanting downward, though in reality they were growing straight up to the blue sky while the rocky soil in which they were rooted was slanting sharply upward.

Jessie and Ki talked little as they moved. The sun was high by the time they passed the fork in the trail where they'd turned the previous day to go along the ledge. A short distance beyond that they stepped across a little rivulet of bubbling, clear water, and began ascending a grade much steeper than any they'd encountered on their earlier visit.

Now they were walking through a thinning forest, and in places where the majestic pines did not grow closely enough together to block their view, they could glimpse even taller peaks. In spite of the coolness that still hung in the air, the unaccustomed steepness of the uphill path soon began to tell on them.

After climbing a short distance their lungs began to strain in the cool, high mountain air. Even though the grade up which they were hiking was still gentle in comparison to the really rugged mountain terrain that surrounded them on all sides, Jessie and Ki were accustomed to the level acres of the Circle Star.

There was a great difference between the two, and they felt its effect on leg muscles and in feet more used to resting in a cow pony's stirrups than in walking up a steep grade. Their aching muscles were reminding them that they were in the tall Sierras instead of their usual prairie surroundings.

Another reminder was furnished by the wildlife they encountered. Some of the small animals that made their homes in the Sierras—chipmunks, ground squirrels, and chickarees—scurried occasionally through the brush beside the trail, and now and then one of them crossed their path, retreating before the advance of alien humanity.

Jays and waxwings flitted from branch to branch in the

pines, the raucous rasping of the jays cutting like a buzz saw through the stillness. Once a porcupine, secure in its barbed coat of quills, stopped on the path ahead of them and stared with bright black eyes at the intruders in its forest domain.

"There doesn't seem to have been much activity up here lately," Ki observed when they stopped in a small clearing to rest for a moment from their steady upward progress. "Or else there've been so many would-be miners around that the animals have gotten used to them."

"They're certainly tame enough," Jessie agreed. "But that could either be because they see people so often that they're used to them, or so seldom that they simply aren't afraid of us."

"It could be either one," Ki agreed. "But we should be getting close to the claims Harney told us about. We passed the place where we turned off the other day a good half-mile back."

"We don't have to be in a hurry," Jessie observed as they started forward again. "Harney will still be waiting for us when we get back."

They'd advanced only another fifty or sixty yards when a heap of fresh dirt just off the trail caught their eyes.

"That must be one of the claims we're looking for," Jessie told Ki. "Somebody's certainly been doing a lot of digging."

Turning off the dimly marked path they'd been following, Jessie and Ki pushed through the brush, sparse at this altitude, to the mounds of earth that had drawn their attention. The soil had come from an excavation made below a narrow ledge of the chalky bedrock that surfaced in a rippling line that ran roughly parallel to the trail. The hole was long and narrow rather than round and symmetrical, as though whoever did the digging had been more interested in the soil close to the surface than in making a deep tunnel.

"This can't be anything but a prospector's claim," Ki told Jessie as they stopped to examine their surroundings.

"But why here, Ki?" she asked. "The ground doesn't look any different around that hole than it does anywhere else. At least if it does I can't tell it."

"That's a question I can't answer," Ki replied. "Unless it's because this is one of the few places we've seen where the bedrock breaks the surface."

"That may well be the reason," Jessie agreed. "But it's obviously a place where somebody was looking for pay dirt, so let's see what we can find."

"Suppose we sample that dirt pile first," Ki suggested. "If we don't find anything in it, I'll cut a piece of branch to dig with and crawl in the hole there to scratch out some fresh dirt that we can look at."

Jessie was already at the dirt pile, using her boot heel to scuff away the loose surface soil and get at the clods below. As she kicked, a bright glint caught her eyes, and she bent forward to pick up the clod within easiest reach and examine it more closely. She prodded it with her fingertips to break the clumsy lump, and as it crumpled she saw the bright glints were metal catching the sunlight that filtered through the pine branches.

"Look, Ki!" she exclaimed. "Unless I'm mistaken, this dirt's got some little flakes of gold in it!"

Ki had been bending down, trying to peer into the hole. He straightened up and hurried to Jessie's side. She opened her hand and, with a fingertip, spread the dirt into a thin layer that covered her palm. The sunlight picked up still more glints of yellow in the ocher-hued soil.

"It does look like gold, at that," he said soberly, the frown on his face echoing itself in his voice. "If it is, this must be a pretty rich vein."

"Perhaps Clem Harney wasn't lying to us after all," Jessie said thoughtfully. "There may be some rich gold deposits in these mountains after all."

Ki shook his head. "I'd find it awfully hard to believe anything that Harney tells us," he answered. "But this really does look like gold to me."

"How can we be sure?" Jessie asked.

"Acid's the only real test I know of that will tell whether these flakes are gold or pyrites," Ki answered. "You remember what Tim Moran told us when we were fighting the cartel's gold dredges down in the Sacramento Valley."

"I remember Tim saying that," Jessie agreed. "But it just happens that we don't have any acid."

"There's another test," Ki went on. "Tim told me about that, too. We can take a handful of this dirt and swirl it in a pan of water to see if these flakes settle to the bottom, the way the placer miners do when they pan a streambed."

"But we don't have either water or a pan to swirl it in," she pointed out.

"We have both at Sierra City," Ki reminded her.

"But that would mean carrying several handfuls of this dirt back there!" Jessie objected. "We don't have to go any farther than that little stream we saw right after we passed that old trail we followed yesterday."

"It's the only thing we can do." Ki shrugged. "Unless you have a better idea. We don't have anything to carry water in, so we'll have to go where the water is."

"Maybe I do have a better idea, Ki," Jessie said, taking her bandanna from her pocket. She started unfolding it. "Here. We can carry almost as much dirt in this as we could in a bucket. We'll just spread it out, heap the dirt in the middle, and I'll fold the corners together to make a kind of basket."

"Good." Ki nodded. "We can just carry it to that little brook we crossed on the way up here and wash the dirt out through the cloth. What's left will be gold ore—if there's any in the dirt, that is."

"Don't worry. There will be," Jessie assured him. "Harney wouldn't have sent us up here unless he was sure we'd find gold. Let's get to work."

Hunkering down beside the dirt pile, they started scoop-ing it up in handfuls, dropping the dirt on the outspread bandanna.

They'd been working only a few seconds when Jessie told Ki, "You know, I see a lot of what looks like gold, even without this dirt being washed."

"Yes, I've noticed that, too. So unless these flakes are bits of pyrites, this really is rich ore."

"Is it possible we've been misjudging Harney, Ki?"

"We won't know that until these flakes are assayed," Ki said. "But I'd guess the chances are against it."

They'd scooped up several more handfuls of the loose dirt from the pile when Ki dumped a fistful of it and sud-denly grasped Jessie's wrist to stop her from dropping the handful she was lifting.

"Just a minute, Jessie," he said. "I see something in that dirt I just dropped that's not a rock. It's metal, but it's not a big flake of gold, either."

Brushing aside the dirt that had trickled into the gap from which he'd just taken a handful, Ki picked up a small metal cylinder. He blew away the few bits of earth that still clung to it and held it out in his palm for Jessie to examine.

"You were right about our misjudging Harney," he told her. "But not in the way you meant. Look at this."

"It's a cap," she said slowly. "A percussion cap from an old-fashioned gun. I can't tell whether it's from a rifle or a pistol, but I certainly know what it is."

"Try shotgun," Ki said. "Look at the size of the cap."

"Yes, of course. A big old muzzle-loader. It'd have to be an old gun, because modern ones use shells."

"No wonder we've been finding these flakes, Jessie. They're real gold, all right. We won't even need to have them assayed to be sure. Harney's salted this hole for his victims to find."

"I've heard about salting claims," Jessie nodded slowly. "Whoever does it loads a shotgun with gold flakes like the ones we've been finding, and aims the gun at whatever

147

piece of earth he wants to salt. Then when he fires, the gold flakes are driven into the dirt like buckshot."

"Exactly." Ki nodded. "And whoever digs into the dirt finds the gold scattered just like it would be if nature had put the flakes there."

"He must've dropped this cap when he reloaded for a second shot," Jessie said, frowning thoughtfully.

"I'm sure that's what happened," Ki agreed. "He may even have fired three loads of gold flakes into the hole and this pile of dirt, because these flakes are pretty thick."

"Well, it looks like we've got our answer, Ki," Jessie said. "There's no use washing more than a handful of this dirt, now that we know what Harney did. We'll just take back enough to show him and convince him that we've fallen for his trick."

Walking downhill was much faster than ascending. Jessie and Ki wasted no time, but moved swiftly down the slope until Sierra City came in sight across the meadow. As they followed the curving trail, and the deserted town's houses could be seen clearly, Jessie suddenly stopped and grabbed Ki's arm as she pointed.

"Harney's last advertisements must have brought him some more sheep to shear," she commented.

Following her pointing finger, Ki saw a light buckboard standing beside the old hotel, a horse still hitched between its shafts.

"I suppose the people are inside talking to him now," she went on. "At least we'll be able to save some of his victims."

They hurried on across the meadow, and were within fifty yards of the old hotel when Clem Harney came out of the door, accompanied by a man and a woman. He was looking from one to the other, his jaw wagging, and did not look in the direction from which Jessie and Ki were approaching.

"Quick!" Jessie said, pointing to the nearest clump of

brush. "Let's not let Harney see us. I'd like to overhear what he tells those people."

Before the trio reached the buggy, Jessie and Ki were shielded, and when Harney turned to gesticulate toward the higher country around the meadow, obviously giving the couple directions, he did not see them. Their conversation lasted for only a few moments, then Harney and the man went inside the building while the woman got up into the buggy and sat down.

"Well, my idea didn't work out," Jessie said. "We may as well go on, Ki. We've got to move sometime."

Jessie and Ki hurried toward the building, and the woman in the buggy must have heard them approaching, for she turned to look at them as they came within a few yards of the buggy. Just at that moment Harney and the man came out, their heads together in conversation. Then, when Jessie and Ki were only a few paces distant, the woman turned to look at them again.

"Well, I do declare!" she exclaimed loudly. "Jessica Starbuck! Why, you're the last person in the world I'd have expected to see up here. But I suppose I really shouldn't be so surprised, since Cornelius and I came up to look because your father's name was in the advertisement we read!"

★

Chapter 14

Instead of replying at once to the woman in the wagon, Jessie said under her breath to Ki, "In case you don't remember her, that's Bettina Van Horn. Her husband, Cornelius, is the man standing there with Harney."

"I can't recall ever meeting her, but whoever she is, she's certainly done a good job of telling Harney who you are," Ki replied in the same low half-whisper Jessie had used.

He was studying Bettina Van Horn unobtrusively. Bettina was a fading blonde who, by the looks of her face, was beginning to run to a bit more than pleasant chubbiness. Though she wore a shapeless brown wrapper that concealed her figure, her fingers were stuffed into thin tan gloves that puffed like small half-cooked sausages, and her round protruding cheeks had the look of partly baked biscuits. She had a button of a chin that made only the smallest bulge in the fleshy neck that seemed a tiny bit too small for the high choker collar of her wrapper.

"Bettina's not the brightest person in the world," Jessie went on. "All that she really cares about is establishing herself in society."

"If that's her purpose, isn't this a strange place for her to be visiting?" Ki frowned.

"Not necessarily, now that I think about it," Jessie said, her words coming slowly and in a thoughtful tone. "Breaking into high social circles is very expensive."

"They need money, then?" Ki asked.

"I'm sure they don't have a great deal," Jessie replied. "At least not by the standards of the elite. Bettina has none of her own, and the Van Horn family is what really rich society people would call poor. I know the best job Cornelius ever had was one that Alex gave him, as an assistant to a shipyard executive. I am surprised to see them here, though."

"They certainly couldn't have had any idea you'd be here."

"Of course not. But the damage has already been done. Now that Harney knows who I am, he'll know why we came here. All we can do is make the best of things and try to settle this without risking gunplay."

While they were having their whispered conversation, Jessie and Ki had kept walking toward the old hotel building. With Bettina's revelation of Jessie's last name, Harney had turned his attention away from Van Horn. He was nodding now and then while Van Horn talked, but his eyes were following Jessie and Ki as they continued to walk toward the building.

Jessie decided her best move was to make no move at all, but to wait for Harney to make the advances. She stopped at the wagon where Bettina Van Horn was sitting.

"Hello, Bettina," she said, her voice as casual as though their encounter was taking place in the drawing room of mutual friends.

"I certainly didn't expect to see you here, Jessie," Bettina replied. "I knew Alex owned the land Mr. Harney's selling gold claims on, but neither Cornelius nor I had any idea you were associated with him."

"I'm not," Jessie replied. "And I'm as surprised to see you here as you are to see me, Bettina. Somehow, I can't see you and Cornelius becoming gold miners."

"Oh, that isn't our idea at all!" Bettina replied quickly. "Cornelius is always looking for investment opportunities,

152

and from what Mr. Harney has been telling us, this seems to be a very promising one."

"I'm afraid promises are about all he has to offer," Jessie said, deciding instantly that the Van Horn's visit could provide her with ammunition to force a showdown with Harney. "Ki and I have discovered that the gold mining claims this man Harney's promoting are nothing but a swindling scheme."

"Swindling!" Bettina gasped. "But he seems like such a nice man!"

"Yes, swindlers usually do seem nice. It's part of their stock in trade," Jessie replied, keeping her eyes on Harney and Van Horn. When Bettina did not reply, Jessie turned to look at her and saw the puzzled look on her face. Then she realized that Bettina hadn't understood her remark and went on, "You wouldn't trust a man who acted surly and unhappy, would you?"

"Of course not!" Bettina exclaimed. Then, understanding at last, she nodded and went on, "But if he's selling your land for you, I don't see how you can call him a swindler, Jessie."

"Harney's not selling my land," Jessie explained. "Ki and I came up here to stop him from using Alex's name in connection with these gold claims he's been advertising in the papers."

"It was your father's name that got Cornelius interested." Bettina frowned. "Do you mean to tell me that Mr. Harney doesn't have any connection with your father's estate or with you either, Jessie?"

"I saw Harney for the first time when Ki and I got here two days ago," Jessie replied. "Before that, I'd never heard of him in connection with Alex except through those newspaper advertisements he was running."

"My goodness!" Bettina gasped. "I had no idea that was the case! If we'd known about it, Cornelius and I wouldn't've come here at all!"

"I came here for only one reason," Jessie went on.

"That is to get this situation straightened out. Ki and I arrived too late to do anything last night, and right now I'm just waiting for Cornelius to finish talking with Harney before I start asking him questions myself."

"Please don't wait on our account, Jessie!" Bettina urged. "I'm sure Cornelius would appreciate it if you took a hand in things right now!"

"I think Mrs. Van Horn has the right idea, Jessie," Ki said quickly. "Isn't it time for you to make the first move, since Harney seems determined to avoid talking to you?"

"Yes, I suppose I'd better." Jessie nodded. "You stay here and keep Bettina company. I'll go break in on the conversation Harney and Cornelius are having."

When Jessie started toward the two men, Harney made a move to leave, but Van Horn grasped him firmly by the arm. Jessie reached the pair and said, "I think it's time you and I had a little talk, Mr. Harney. I hadn't planned to say anything just yet, but now that you know who I am—"

"And that was a shoddy trick to play, Jessie Starbuck! I'm not sure what you're implying, but I don't have anything to hide!" Harney blustered.

"I may not agree with you about that," Jessie replied. "Ki and I went up to the claims you told us about. Not the ones we looked at earlier, which were useless because the gold is in a quartz formation. These we looked at today had been salted."

"Now, I deny that totally and completely!" Harney said loudly. "I told you the truth about the claims that had quartziferous ore in them! The ones you saw today produce free gold!"

"You didn't say anything to me about the gold being in a quartz stratum!" Van Horn broke in. "I may never have worked a claim myself, but anyone who grew up in California during the gold rush days knows the difference between free gold and gold in a quartz formation!"

"You haven't any business interfering in this discussion between Miss Starbuck and me!" Harney retorted. "And in

154

any case, you haven't any cause to get upset. So far, you haven't passed a penny over to me."

"That's not your fault!" Van Horn snapped. "You certainly tried hard enough to get me to buy those claims you're offering sight unseen. No wonder you were so insistent on me and Bettina staying over tonight and putting off any more discussion until later! You probably intended to take us out tomorrow and show us the ones Jessie says are salted!"

Jessie thought to herself, perhaps the Van Horns being here will give us just the right lever we need to settle this thing quickly. She spoke up, "Cornelius, if you'll quit arguing with Mr. Harney long enough for me to get a word in, I'd like to get to the root of this argument."

"What do you consider that to be, Jessie?" Van Horn asked.

"Whether he has any real right to be selling claims at all," Jessie replied. "This land belongs to me now, and I want him to prove to me that he and Alex had an agreement allowing him to sell mining claims."

"You don't think he has an agreement?" Van Horn frowned.

"Knowing how my father handled his business affairs, I have a very strong suspicion that any contract he might've signed regarding mineral rights limited this man to working the mines himself after Alex had approved his mining plans."

"That's nonsense!" Harney broke in. "You don't think I'm a big enough fool to be a claims pirate, do you? I wouldn't be advertising these claims for sale in the newspapers unless I'd worked out a deal with your father."

"Then you won't mind producing the original agreement, will you?" Jessie smiled. "Not a copy, mind you. I want to see my father's signature. And I might as well tell you now, Mr. Harney, I know Alex's signature as well as I know my own."

"Naturally, I don't carry documents of that kind around

155

with me in my pocket," Harney said. "The agreement Alex Starbuck signed is in my safe, inside. I'll have to get it."

"If you're telling me the truth, then you won't mind Ki going with you while you get it, will you?" Jessie asked.

"I'll go with him, if you want me to, Jessie," Van Horn volunteered.

"Thank you, Cornelius, but I'd rather Ki went," Jessie replied. "I think he's had a little more experience than you in handling slippery customers such as Mr. Harney seems to be." Turning, she called, "Ki! Will you give me a hand here for a minute, please?"

When Ki started toward them in response to Jessie's call, Harney said, "You don't need to have me escorted just to go into the house, Miss Starbuck. Even if I wanted to run, there's not much of anyplace to run to around here."

"Even so, I'll feel better if Ki goes with you," Jessie said. She turned to Ki and went on, "Just keep an eye on him while he opens his safe and gets out the agreement he made with Alex."

"Of course," Ki nodded.

"It'll only take a few minutes to read the agreement. If he concedes that it no longer has any standing, I might be willing to let him go without having him arrested." Facing Harney again, she went on, "Well, Mr. Harney? Is freedom better than prison, or do you intend to keep arguing? I'll warn you, my patience is wearing thin."

"I guess you've got the winning hand," Harney said reluctantly. "I'll make a deal with you, Miss Starbuck."

As Ki and Harney went into the old hotel building, Van Horn said, "Bettina and I will have to talk about this new development, Jessie. We naturally thought that the Starbuck interests were associated with Harney in this gold claims venture after we saw the advertisements that mentioned Alex's name. It's a bit disturbing to find that Harney's handling it by himself."

"Of course," Jessie nodded. "Go ahead and talk with her. But don't count on the golden promises that I'm sure

Harney made to you. As soon as this mix-up over mineral rights is settled, I'm going to forget all about mining this property, now or in the future."

Van Horn stepped over to the wagon, where he and his wife began talking in low voices, their heads close together. Jessie waited patiently, flicking her eyes over the vista that unfolded before her. She found in it something as comforting as the vast prairie that surrounded the Circle Star.

There was a similar serenity in the towering peaks, half-hidden by the forest of tall pines that began beyond the green mountain meadow. Though the wind-riffled surface of the lake at the meadow's edge was only partly visible, she could watch the play of the light late-morning breeze as it created low ripples in the blue water. The total stillness of the peaceful scene contributed to the sudden sense of well-being that came over Jessie, in spite of the problems that she knew lay ahead.

Then her peaceful mood was shattered when the hard muzzle of a rifle pressed into her back and Harney's voice broke the quiet of the late afternoon.

"You just stand still, Miss Starbuck," he said. His tone was not the one he'd used before but was as hard as the muzzle of the rifle that was jammed into her backbone. "And don't look for any help from that Chink of yours—I took care of him. Now if you do just what I tell you, you won't get hurt."

Jessie's first thought was of Ki. She had no illusions about Harney, only regret for having misjudged his character.

Her next impulse came instinctively, to use the backward *kansetsu-geri* kick that Ki had taught her to sweep the rifle from Harney's hands. Then she realized that his trigger finger's reaction could be faster than her own move. Her decision to wait for a better opportunity came almost as swiftly as the thought of resistance.

"What do you want me to do?" she asked.

157

"Call your friends and tell them to join us," Harney said. "I don't want to have to kill you or them, but I damned sure will if you try any funny tricks on me."

There was a strain of irrational violence implicit in Harney's nervous tone, and Jessie knew when she heard it that she'd made the right decision.

"I'll make you a trade," she offered.

"What kind of trade?" Harney asked, his voice even edgier than before.

"I'll do whatever you tell me to," she said soothingly. "But first you must tell me what you've done with Ki."

"I'll tell you this much," Harney replied. "He's all right. He's just locked up in a safe place."

Although she realized she was pusing her luck, Jessie continued to stall. She asked, "What do you plan to do with us?"

"You'll find out soon enough, but don't worry. I'm not going to kill anybody unless I have to," Harney said. "Now quit stalling and call those two up here!"

Harney's voice was even edgier than before, and Jessie knew she would be unable to delay any longer. Raising her voice, she called to the Van Horns, "Cornelius! Bettina! Perhaps you'd like to join me and Mr. Harney for a moment!"

Without questioning Jessie's request, Van Horn helped his wife down from the seat of the wagon, and they walked up to where Jessie and Harney were standing. Jessie felt the pressure of the rifle muzzle leave her back for the first time as Harney swung the gun to cover the new arrivals.

"Just do what I tell you and you won't get hurt," he said. "Now, I want all three of you to walk in front of me. We'll go inside, and you walk across the room to the door on the other side. Go on through it down the hall until you get to the end. Stop there and I'll tell you what to do next."

"Do what he says," Jessie told them calmly. "I don't know what Mr. Harney intends to do with us, but he's holding the gun, and all three of us had better obey him."

158

"Now you're showing some sense," Harney grated. "Listen to Miss Starbuck's advice, and you'll be all right."

With Jessie leading the way, the three captives moved into the old hotel building, passed through the big room that had been its lobby to a door that opened in the opposite wall. It led them into a narrow hallway.

Jessie walked slowly down the long corridor, passing a half-dozen closed doors, to the end of the hall. She stopped in front of a door secured with a hasp and massive padlock.

"Here," Harney said, handing Jessie a key. "Unlock the padlock, give me back the key, then open the door a crack and tell the Chinaman you're coming through it."

"If you mean Ki, he's Japanese, not Chinese," Jessie said coolly as she put the key into the padlock. "But I'll tell him to stand aside, out of the way."

Jessie inserted the key in the padlock and passed both lock and key back to Bettina before she pushed the door open. The room beyond showed only a dense blackness, which her eyes could not penetrate.

"Ki!" she called. "Are you there?"

"Yes, Jessie. I know you'd—" Ki began.

Jessie cut him short. "Be quiet and listen to me, Ki! Harney's holding us out here in the hall with a rifle. He's sending us inside with you. Don't do anything rash. If you do, he'll shoot."

His voice sounding strangely distorted, Ki replied, "I understand, Jessie. I won't do anything to put you in danger."

"All right!" Harney commanded when Ki stopped speaking. "Go on inside, all three of you."

"Do you mind telling me—" Jessie began.

"Shut up!" Harney snapped. "Just do what you're told!"

Jessie fell silent and stepped through the door. She noticed as she passed through it that it and the walls of its casing were unusually thick, but she was more anxious to see Ki than she was in taking note of such incidentals.

Ki was peering at her, his eyes squinted into an even

narrower slant than usual. In the gloom of the windowless room she found herself in, Jessie could see his face only dimly. She got only a brief glimpse, though. The footsteps of Cornelius and Bettina Van Horn sounded behind her, then the door banged shut and the gloom suddenly became total darkness.

"Ki?" Jessie called.

His voice sounding as though he was only inches away, Ki replied, "I'm right here, Jessie. And I'm all right, so don't waste time worrying about me."

"Okay," Jessie answered. "But do you have any idea where on earth we are?"

"Certainly. I've been here long enough to work it all out in my mind," Ki said. "This room must have been planned to hold ice. I'd imagine the people who built this hotel were counting on cutting the thick ice that must form on that lake in the winter and storing it in here."

"Of course!" Jessie replied. "I noticed how thick the door is when I came in. And I suppose the walls are just as thick, then? Or have you tried to find out?"

"Naturally I have!" Ki answered. "And your guess is a good one, because I reached the same conclusion myself. From what I can tell by feeling them, the walls must be made of tongue-and-groove lumber, and I imagine that since it was supposed to be an oversized ice-chest, they're double walls with a thick layer of sawdust between them."

"You have your *tanto,* don't you?" Jessie asked.

"Certainly," Ki said. "I've been trying to cut through the wall ever since Harney locked me in. He tricked me into starting through the door ahead of him by saying his safe was in here, then when I stepped inside, he gave me a push that sent me sprawling. Before I could get up and locate the door again, he'd slammed it shut and locked it."

"We've got to get out, though!" Van Horn exclaimed. "If your conclusions are right, this room's virtually airtight, and with four of us in it, we'll use up the air very fast!"

"That occurred to me, too," Ki said. "I tried my *tanto*—that's a knife, if you don't know—but it doesn't work very fast. There's no place to begin cutting. I've been chipping away, but I can't make much progress trying to cut through this double-thick lumber."

"How about your *shuriken*?" Jessie suggested. "They have toothed edges—couldn't you use them like a saw?"

"I hadn't thought of that," Ki said. "But it'll be worth a try. I'll see if they're any better than the knife."

There was a sound of metal on wood as Ki began working with one of the razor-edged throwing disks. The sound continued for several minutes, then Ki spoke again.

"This is better than the knife, but it's still too slow. If I'm right about this room being double-walled, it'll take a day to make any kind of impression on this thick wood. We'd all be dead by then!"

"But somebody's got to figure out a way to get us free!" Bettina Van Horn wailed. "I'm far too young to die!"

Chapter 15

"Stop that at once, Bettina!" Jessie snapped as Bettina began sobbing after her outburst. "This isn't the time or place for you to start feeling sorry for yourself! Can't you realize that if we don't get out of here fast, we'll suffocate?"

Unexpectedly, Cornelius Van Horn spoke up in support of Jessie's remark. "Jessie's right, Bettina," he said. "Stop thinking only of yourself and start trying to help!"

Shocked into silence, Bettina stifled her sobs and asked, "How long do you think we can last if we don't get the door open, Jessie?"

"I don't know," Jessie replied. "I'd have to measure the size of this room to work out how much air it holds, and there's not any way to do that without light."

"I paced off the room and made a guess at its size right after Harney locked me in here," Ki volunteered. "It's about eight by eight feet, and I can't touch the ceiling even when I stand on tiptoe, so I don't know how high it is. My guess is eight feet, though."

"I imagine that's what it would be," Jessie agreed. "Equal in all dimensions." She calculated rapidly in her head. "That means about five hundred cubic feet of air. Not a great deal for the four of us, if I remember what I learned in school about how much air we need per minute."

"I gave myself between two and three hours of breathing," Ki said quickly. "If you divide that by four, it's easy to see that we've got to work fast."

"Do you think we can make it, Ki?" Jessie asked, her voice quite calm.

"We can if we keep at it," Ki replied. "We'll be all right if we can just make a hole big enough to let some fresh air in. This room is almost totally airtight."

"Tell us what to do, then," Van Horn said. He seemed less fearful now.

Jessie answered Van Horn before Ki could speak. "Right at the moment the best thing you and Bettina and I can do is to sit down, stay absolutely still, and stop talking, so we won't be using extra air," she told him.

"Jessie's right," Ki agreed. He was still working at the wall beside the door, the sound of his *shuriken* sounding very loud in the small, dark room as he kept working on the tough wooden wall.

"You heard what Ki said, Bettina," Van Horn told his still-sobbing wife. "Now let's do it. Stop your foolish crying and settle down. All you're doing is wasting precious air with those big gulping sobs of yours."

"Why, Nelius!" Bettina cried. "You've never spoken to me like that in your life before!"

"If he hasn't, it's about time he did, then," Jessie told her coldly. "Do as Cornelius says, Bettina! And do it now!"

With a few more sobs and a final loud, shuddering inhalation, Bettina reduced her cries to low-keyed whimpers.

During the conversation between Cornelius and Bettina, Ki had continued to work at the wall with his *shuriken*. After they'd fallen silent, Jessie listened for what seemed a long time to the steady rasp, rasp, rasp of the throwing blade Ki was using. At last curiosity overcame her awareness that she'd be wasting precious air and she spoke to him.

"Are you making any progress, Ki?"

"Some, I guess. It'd go faster if these points were closer together, like the teeth of a saw, but I'm managing to cut a little bit deeper all the time. I've got a groove that's about a quarter of an inch deep, as far as I can tell just by feeling the tip of my *shuriken*."

"How much longer do you think it will take to cut through?"

"It's hard to tell. Remember, I don't even know how thick these boards are. If they're as thick as I suspect, an inch or more, it's going to take a long, long time just to cut an opening on this inside wall."

"It's harder work than I thought it would be," Jessie said. "But it's our only chance to get out."

"I know," Ki replied. "And what's got to be done after we cut a hole in the first wall's going to take even longer."

"You think the second wall might be made from thicker boards?"

"No. But if I'm right, there'll be a thick layer of sawdust between these two walls. That'll have to be taken out before I can even reach the outer wall. It'll take us quite a while to get out enough sawdust to keep it out of my way. Then I'll be working in a hole when I start on the outside wall, so I won't be able to move my hands as freely."

"That hadn't occurred to me," Jessie said. "But the air in here's still a lot fresher than I thought it would be with four of us breathing it. Remember, though, the more we talk the more air we'll use."

In the silence that followed Jessie's reminder, the only sound that filled the darkness was the continued rasping of Ki's *shuriken* sawing at the wall. The harsh grating of the throwing blade's sawtoothed edge was a constant reminder of the limited time that remained to the four captives. After the noise had gone on without interruption for what seemed an interminable time, Bettina started sobbing again, though this time she was obviously trying to muffle her sniffling cries.

"Get hold of yourself, Bettina!" Cornelius urged. "Can't

you understand that we're all in the same fix, and you're the only one who's acting like a baby?"

"I—I just can't help it!" Bettina managed to say between her gulping sobs. "It's my fault we came up here, too! We'd have been better off if we'd just stayed home!"

Trying to cheer her up, Jessie said, "Bettina, none of this is our fault. Harney's the one to blame. He's responsible for getting all of us up here, even if it was for different reasons."

"That doesn't cheer me up very much, Jessie," Bettina whimpered. "I still feel like I'm to blame. Oh, if I just had a gun, I'd shoot myself and get it all over with!"

"Now that's—" Jessie began, then stopped short. After a moment's thought, she went on, "Ki, what Bettina just said reminded me that I do have a gun. And it's pretty obvious by now that no matter how hard you work, you're not going to be able to cut a hole in that wall fast enough to get us out before we suffocate."

"I've been facing that fact for the last several minutes," Ki admitted. "Ever since Bettina started worrying. And I'd forgotten your Colt, too."

"Do you think it'll work?" Jessie asked.

"It's hard to judge," Ki answered, his voice thoughtful. "Shooting in the dark, not being exactly sure of where the door hasp's located—well, it's a chance, at best. But this wood is too tough to cut easily with the only tools we have, and the boards are so thick that I'm just not making much progress."

"Then it's time to stop being careful and gamble," Jessie went on. "If I try to shoot the hasp off that door and fail, the shots will burn up a lot of air and fill this little place with smoke and powder fumes. But if I succeed, we'll be free in just a few seconds."

"What bothers me is that your pistol slugs might not be able to smash through these thick boards," Ki said.

Though Jessie could not see his face in the dark room, she could read the concern in Ki's voice. She replied, "I'd rather have a rifle, of course. But all I've got is the Colt."

"Then let's try it," Ki said. "Can you find such a small target in the dark?"

"Do you remember how high the hasp is?" Jessie asked him.

"I think so. It was just about level with the middle of my chest."

Cornelius Van Horn spoke for the first time since his scolding words to his wife. "Try it, for God's sake!" he urged. "Anything's better than this slow suffocation!"

"Neely's right, Jessie," Bettina said in a small, unhappy voice. "Go ahead and try."

"You'll have to help me, Ki," Jessie said as she drew the Colt. "Stand by the edge of the door and I'll use the middle of your chest to locate my target area."

In the stillness that settled over the dark room, Jessie heard the slight rustle of Ki's movement as he abandoned his efforts to cut through the wall and moved to the door. She stepped up to join him, reaching out to feel the wall and running her fingertips across the heavy planks until her hand encountered Ki's muscular arm.

He was standing with his back pressed against the wall, and when Jessie felt his arm she shifted the Colt from her right hand to her left and began running her fingertips along its surface. She moved her hand horizontally, slowly and with infinite care, feeling each almost infinitesimally small crack where the thick boards butted together, until she encountered the larger crack where the stout door met the jamb.

"I've located the edge of the door now," she told Ki. "Slip along the wall until you feel my hand. I want to be sure that I get the Colt's muzzle at the right height."

A slight rustling noise broke the silence as Ki obeyed, then she felt his chest pressing against the hand she was holding to the wall. Ki stopped when he encountered Jessie's hand.

"Yes," he said. "That feels just about the right height.

I'll move out of your way, then you can shoot whenever you're ready."

Jessie waited until she heard Ki's back brushing the wall as he stepped aside, then raised her Colt and pressed its cold muzzle at the spot where she'd been holding her finger.

"I hope this is right," she said. In spite of the doubt her words had indicated, her voice was calm and level. "That hasp is only a couple of inches wide, as I remember, so I don't have much leeway. But it's the best I can do on the first try. If I miss, we've still got four more chances."

Slitting her eyes in anticipation of the muzzle blast, Jessie triggered the Colt. For a split second the blackness gave way to the jet of brightness that spurted from the pistol's muzzle as the reverberating boom of the shot echoed around the small, tightly closed room, and for the fraction of a second before the echoes started, Jessie could hear the sullen growl of the slug plowing into the sturdy wall.

Then the sepulchral silence that followed the shot hung heavily in the air and the acrid scent of burned powder crept across the tiny chamber. Jessie broke the silence.

"I don't see any light," she said, her voice levelly calm. "That means the slug didn't go through the wall. I hope it was the hasp on the outside that stopped it."

"Try again," Ki urged.

"I intend to," Jessie said, sliding the Colt's muzzle a fraction of an inch below the spot where the first slug had crashed into the door crack.

Again the partly smothered muzzle blast flashed, and again the echoes of the shot filled the room. The sharp throat-burning smell of exploded gunpowder settled down and set Jessie and Ki to coughing. A moment later, the coughs of Bettina and Cornelius joined those of Ki and Jessie.

"Oh, this is terrible," Bettina gasped. "I can hardly breathe!"

"Be glad you can breathe at all," Van Horn said between coughs. "Get close to the floor, it'll be better."

At the door, Ki was pushing hard. The sturdy boards seemed to give a bit as he shoved his shoulder against them, and he said to Jessie, "I'm sure that hasp has loosened up, Jessie! Try another shot!"

Jessie triggered the Colt for the third time. A clank of metal echoed as the boom of the gunshot faded, and Ki resumed his pushing at the door. He called, "Cornelius, come add your weight to mine! I think Jessie's hit the target this time!"

By now the powder smoke and acrid fumes hung heavily in the little chamber, and all four of its occupants were coughing and wheezing. Van Horn reached the door, and when he added his weight to Ki's there was a sudden splintering noise. The heavy door opened with a creaking sound that was drowned in the sharp crash as the door swung against the corridor wall, allowing daylight and fresh air to flood into the room.

"You did it, Jessie!" Ki exclaimed, his usual calm deserting him. "Look at those grooves in the doorjamb! Every bullet went in the right direction!"

Blinking to clear her eyes of the tears created by the thick cloud of powder smoke that still hung in the air, Jessie looked at the closely spaced grooves made in the jamb and matched on the edge of the door that marked the path of her bullets. The slugs themselves, polished mirror-bright, were embedded in the splintered wood, and the hasp with its heavy padlock hanging from it was still swinging back and forth.

"Call it Starbuck luck," Jessie told him, her eyes fixed on the swinging hasp. "If any of those shots had been an inch higher or lower, we'd still be inside."

By now Cornelius and Bettina had groped their way through the thick, acrid smoke that had filled the small chamber and were coming into the hall.

169

"Thank heavens you got us out of that, Jessie," Cornelius said between coughs. "For a while, I wasn't sure any of us were going to come out of there!"

"I was scared half to death!" Bettina added. She turned to her husband and went on, "Cornelius, if we leave right now, we can get back to Truckee before dark. I don't know whether there's a train out of there tonight, but if there isn't, we'll go back on the first one tomorrow."

"No, Bettina!" Jessie said quickly. "You and Cornelius will have to stay here until Harney comes back."

"Well, I certainly don't see why!" Bettina snapped. "You haven't any call to be giving us orders, anyhow, Jessie. If your name hadn't been in that newspaper ad, Nelius and I never would have come here!"

"Perhaps not. But you absolutely cannot leave until Harney gets back," Jessie said firmly.

"I'd like to know why!" Bettina said.

"Yes, so would I," Van Horn added quickly. "After what's happened to us, I don't want to stay here any longer than we have to."

Ki spoke for the first time since their liberation from the locked room. "I think I understand why Jessie said that. She wants Harney to see your horse and wagon when he gets back."

"What makes you think he's coming back?" Van Horn asked.

"Think about it for a moment and you'll see why," Jessie said. "Harney is going to be sure that all four of us are dead, still locked up in that room where he put us. If he doesn't see your horse and wagon, he'll know we've managed to get out."

"He'll know that soon enough, anyhow," Van Horn put in.

"Of course." Jessie nodded. "But not until we've captured him. And you won't have long to wait. I don't think he's gone very far."

"Wherever he went, he didn't take his horse," Ki said as

he turned back from counting the animals grazing in the meadow. "My guess is that he's gone to look at those abandoned claims."

"Why?" Bettina frowned. "What earthly good would it do him to look at a few holes in the ground?"

"He'll be looking for the deepest one to throw our bodies into," Jessie said matter-of-factly. "And a place like one of those abandoned claims up on the mountainside would be ideal."

"To throw our—" Bettina began. Then she stopped short, her mouth fell open wide, and she stared at Jessie and Ki with a horror-struck expression forming on her face.

"Of course," Ki said, "if someone found our bodies buried in an abandoned mine shaft they'd assume we were caught in a cave-in. They'd know we'd been murdered if there were bullet holes in our bodies."

When Ki stopped and neither Bettina nor Cornelius spoke, Jessie picked up where Ki had left off.

"What Ki's been trying to tell you," she said, "is that Harney intended for all four of us to die of suffocation."

"That's what he had in mind." Ki nodded. "But now his original scheme won't work."

"What a gruesome thought!" Bettina exclaimed. She turned to her husband and asked, "Do you believe that Jessie and Ki are right, Nelius?"

"I'm afraid they are," Van Horn said soberly. "If we'd suffocated in that room the way he planned for us to, there wouldn't have been any bullet holes in our bodies. I suppose that's why he didn't shoot us."

"Yes." Ki nodded. "And if Jessie's right, he'll be coming back to haul our bodies up there and bury us before too long."

"Instead of us trying to follow him, though, all we have to do is wait for him to come back," Jessie went on. "The thing for us to do is for Ki and me to get our rifles, then all of us will hide in one of these abandoned houses. When

171

Harney shows up, we'll capture him and take him to Truckee and hand him over to the sheriff."

"I—I guess I understand now," Bettina stammered. "But to think about a cold-blooded scheme like that just chills me to my very marrow!"

"None of the rest of us like it any better," Jessie said. "But let's just be thankful that we got away before Harney had a chance to carry out his ugly scheme. And now that you understand what's been going on, Bettina, please just do what we say without arguing about it."

"All right, Jessie," Bettina agreed. "Just tell us what you want us to do, and we'll do it. Won't we, Nelius?"

"Of course," Van Horn agreed. "But I'm afraid I don't have a rifle, or even a pistol, so I can't be of much help."

Jessie looked thoughtfully at the trail that she and Ki had taken that morning and said, "I suppose Harney will come down that trail, but I'm not sure. What do you think, Ki?"

"I think he will, too, so I suggest that you go into the old hotel with Bettina and her husband. Get on the second floor, where you'll have a better view. I'll go partway up the trail, and when Harney comes back we'll have him in a cross fire."

"Simple plans are always the best," Jessie said. "That's what we'll do, then. I'll run down to the house where we're staying and get my rifle. It'll only take a minute."

Within two or three minutes, Jessie returned carrying her Winchester. Ki said, "I'll start now. You can handle things at this end."

Jessie nodded, and as Ki started away she said to the Van Horns, "Come on, Bettina and Cornelius. We can get ourselves located while Ki's moving into place along the trail. Harney might be on his way back by now, and we want to be ready when he shows up."

Ki began trotting toward the lake, following the trail that would take him up the mountainside. Jessie led Bettina and Cornelius into the old hotel. When they were inside

172

she said, "I think if you two get into one of the rooms downstairs here, you'll be all right. Pick out one on the other side of the building, and stay there no matter what happens. I'll find a place upstairs in a room with a window overlooking the trail."

Bettina and Cornelius nodded their understanding and moved off. Jessie hurried to the stairway at the end of the hall opposite the room where they'd been confined and went up to the second floor. It took her only a few minutes to discover the location she'd been hoping for, a room with windows that overlooked the lake and the trail up the mountainside. She opened one of the windows and found that she had a clear view of the winding trail as it zig-zagged up the steep slope beyond the lake.

Checking her Winchester to make sure there was a shell in the chamber, she drew up a chair and placed it beside the window. Then she sat down to wait.

★

Chapter 16

This was not the first vigil of its kind that Jessie had kept. She knew from past experience the dangers of letting herself be hypnotized by keeping her eyes fixed too long on the same spot, and she moved her head often, shifting her attention to different zones of the area she was watching.

Along the portion of the trail visible to her, and on the slopes and meadow through which the faint trace ran, there were places where thick clusters of pine trees grew along the zigzagging uphill path, and on the meadow patches of chamisal, the thin-stemmed brush of the Sierras. Both hid sections of the trail from view, and Jessie concentrated on the clear areas, knowing that she'd spot Harney easily between the patches of cover.

Soon after she'd settled into position at the window, Jessie spotted Ki emerging from one of these blind spots and scrambling up the steep bluff beside the trail to find his own hiding place. She noted in her mind the spot that Ki had chosen, a wide swath of barren slope flanked on each side by dense undergrowth, with the dark-golden trunks of the stately pines rising above it.

She memorized the terrain around it, not only to be sure that she would not endanger Ki's life by firing a bullet that might whistle into Ki's hiding place, but to be equally sure that she would be able to tell at once when Harney had moved far enough along the trail on his return to Sierra

City to be caught between herself and Ki.

Although Jessie had her full share of patience, and knew that Ki had inherited the Oriental ability to wait motionless for long periods of time, she soon found herself wishing for her lonely vigil to end. The afternoon was well along by now, and across the vestigial trail the sun was beginning to cast the shadows of the high peaks that rose beyond the mountains' flanks. Jessie concentrated on the terrain, and controlled her growing impatience. When she heard the scraping of feet on the floor behind her, she swiveled instinctively, the rifle leveled toward the door.

"Don't shoot, Jessie!" Cornelius Van Horn said quickly.

"I won't, don't worry," Jessie replied sharply. "What are you doing here, though? I told you and Bettina to find a room and stay in it."

"I know," he said, "but when we opened the door to one of the rooms upstairs we found something you'd better look at, since Ki's not here."

"You know I'm watching for Harney and can't leave here!" Jessie said. "Whatever you've found will just have to wait."

"Well, I guess that'll be all right," Van Horn said. "We found a dead man, and I don't guess a few minutes is going to matter to him."

"A dead man?" Jessie frowned.

"That's right." He nodded. "His head's all bloody, and he's stretched out on a bed. I thought you ought to know about him."

"Did you ever see the man before?" Jessie asked.

Van Horn shook his head. "No. And I can't tell you much about him except that he's got on the kind of rough clothes a workman might wear. There's so much blood on his head that I couldn't make out anything special about his face."

"I suppose I'd better go look," Jessie said. "But since we've been up here, Ki and I haven't seen anybody except—" She broke off, her eyes widening, and went on,

"I think I know who he is. Show me the way to that room."

"What about Harney?"

"Ki's hiding out there, watching the trail. I can leave him to take care of Harney."

Van Horn nodded and turned toward the door. Jessie followed him. He led the way through the corridor, then across the main room and up a flight of stairs at the rear. A long, door-lined corridor stretched in front of them. Near its end, Bettina Van Horn stood, her arms wrapped around her body as though she was embracing herself. Even at a distance Jessie could see the whites of her bulging eyes.

When she saw Jessie and Cornelius, Bettina started running toward them. "Thank goodness you got here at last!" she gasped. "I've never been so frightened before in my life! Standing watch over a dead man is—"

"Shut up, Bettina!" Cornelius snapped. "Dead men can't hurt anyone! Now, get hold of yourself and stop acting like a scared child!"

"Why, Nelius!" Bettina stammered. "You—you've never talked to me like this before today!"

"Perhaps if I had you wouldn't be acting like such a ninny now," her husband retorted. "Just stay right where you are and let Jessie and me get past you."

Bettina moved aside and Jessie brushed by, through the door at which Bettina had been standing. The only furniture in the small room was a dresser and bed. Matt Bolton lay on the bed, and it took Jessie only a quick glance to see that Van Horn had not exaggerated. Bolton's head was completely covered with dried blood, and the front of his shirt was stained red as well.

Ignoring what was obvious, Jessie stepped up to the bed and lifted Bolton's wrist. To her surprise, she felt a slow but steady pulse.

"He's still alive!" she said over her shoulder to Van Horn. "Go get some water, quick!"

"But where—" he began.

"Try the kitchen," Jessie snapped. "If you have to, take

a bucket up to the lake and fill it! Just hurry!"

"But if Harney sees me—" he managed to say before Jessie cut him short again.

"Ki will take care of Harney!" she told him. "Go find some water like I told you to!"

Van Horn hurried away and, after a moment of hesitation, Betina followed him. Jessie kept her finger on Matt Bolton's pulse, which had not varied since she'd first felt it. After what seemed to her an eternity, Van Horn came back, carrying a bucket.

"Here's the water," he said. "Where do you want it?"

"Put it right by the bed here," she told him. "And take your coat off."

"My coat?" he asked, his jaw dropping. "Why on earth—"

"Please don't ask so many questions! Just do it!"

His eyes fixed on Jessie with a puzzled frown, Van Horn did as she'd told him.

"Do you have a pocketknife?" Jessie asked.

"A little penknife is all I—"

"Let me have it," Jessie broke in.

Still mystified, Van Horn handed Jessie the knife he'd taken from his pocket. She opened it, stepped up to him, pulled the fabric of his shirt up at the shoulder, and struck the knife into the sleeve at the shoulder seam.

"Wait a minute!" Van Horn protested. "You're not going to cut—"

Jessie was already cutting along the shoulder seam. She lifted Van Horn's arm and finished her cut, then pulled the sleeve off his arm. Stepping closer to the bed, she dipped the shirtsleeve into the bucket and, without stopping to wring it out, began mopping the unconscious Bolton's face.

For a moment, her attentions had no results, then Bolton stirred and his eyes opened. He tried to sit up, but Jessie pushed his head back down.

"Lie still," she told him. "Wait until you feel better."

178

"I feel all right except that I've got one hell of a head-ache," Matt said. "Harney! He shot me, damn him! Where's he, Jessie?"

"Up on the mountainside getting our graves ready," Jessie replied grimly. "Don't worry about him."

"Graves?" Bolton gasped. "Jessie, what's going on here? Who's this fellow with you? And what's happened?"

"I'll tell you about everything later," she replied. "When did Harney shoot you? And why?"

Looking around, Bolton replied, "It—it's daylight, so if today's tomorrow, I guess it was yesterday."

"It was yesterday when you were starting back to your timber stand," Jessie said. "Now tell me why he shot you."

"I was getting ready to leave when Harney told me he wanted to talk to me," Bolton said. His face drew into a puzzled frown as he tried to make sense of the time sequences. "He told me he needed my help, and I asked him what for. Then he begun telling me how he'd rigged up the gold claims and that we could make a lot of money if I'd just help him. But I said I didn't want any part of it, and that's when he shot me. That's all I remember."

"It's easy to figure out the rest," Jessie said. "He dragged you up here so Ki and I wouldn't stumble over your body, except that you weren't dead, and Harney thought you were." She stopped and shook her head. "I'm beginning to sound as confused as you do, Matt. But there's nothing for you to worry about. Just lie still until you get your strength back."

"Who's this fellow with you?" Bolton frowned.

"His name's Cornelius Van Horn," Jessie said. Turning to Cornelius, she went on, "You stay here and look after Matt. I've got to get back to that window. Ki's out on the meadow somewhere, and Harney's probably starting down the mountain on his way back here by now."

"I still don't understand," Matt Bolton protested. "If—"

"You will," Jessie promised. She turned to Van Horn and went on, "Try to tell Matt what's gone on. I'll send

Bettina to stay with you. Don't worry about a thing. Ki and I will take care of Harney when he shows up."

As Jessie hurried back to the room overlooking the meadow, she kept expecting to see Bettina Van Horn, but when she crossed the lobby Bettina was nowhere in sight. Well aware that her time was running out, Jessie shrugged and returned to her lookout post.

Ki was nowhere in sight when she looked out the window, but Jessie had not expected him to be. She knew that he'd found some spot on the meadow where, with *ninja* skill, he'd faded into the landscape. She turned her attention to the darkly dappled slope beyond the lake, where the brush was thinner, and through the topmost twigs of elderberry and buttonbush she saw a flash of alien color suddenly appear between two stands of pines.

In a moment Clem Harney came into sight, making his way down to the meadow. Harney was still some distance away from the nearest spot where Jessie judged that Ki was most likely to be waiting. She did nothing but watch as the swindler moved along the trail.

If Jessie had not been accustomed to Ki's *ninja* movements, she would not have seen him when he suddenly appeared from nowhere. Even after she'd spotted him by the occasional flicks of movement that betrayed his presence as he descended the slope behind Harney, it was difficult to see him. Though she knew what to expect, Jessie caught only the most fleeting glimpses of Ki, a flash of movement now and then as he dodged from one spot of cover to the next, until he was only a dozen or so yards behind Harney.

Straightening in her chair, Jessie rested the muzzle of her Winchester on the windowsill as Harney drew closer in his passage across the meadow. She searched the trail with her eyes, but at some point Ki had disappeared. Then she looked back at Harney just in time to see him turn in the center of the trail. He was bringing up his rifle as he spun around.

Out of the corner of her eye Jessie caught the hint of some kind of motion, but it was too fleeting for her to tell what had moved, or if indeed there'd been any movement at all. By this time Harney had shouldered his rifle, his head bending to put his eyes in line with the weapon's sights.

Jessie was convinced now that Ki had somehow made a mistake and had given Harney some kind of hint that he was being followed. She shouldered her Winchester, quickly lined the sights up. Her finger was tightening on the trigger when, almost at Harney's feet, a porcupine waddled slowly out of a clump of brush that stood close to the trail. Jessie let her trigger finger relax when she saw Harney lower his rifle muzzle as the porcupine made its unhurried way across the trail.

Harney watched the porky's slow progress for a moment. Then, with his rifle butt settled back into the crook of his elbow, he turned and resumed walking toward the settlement again. For a moment Jessie watched him, then an almost invisible movement in the low brush beside the trail caught her eye, and she saw Ki slipping along on all fours parallel to the trail, his body only inches above the ground.

With a small sigh of relief, Jessie let the muzzle of the Winchester drop until it rested on the windowsill again. She waited until Harney had gotten to within a dozen yards of the old hotel building, then brought her rifle up once more, covering him.

"Stop right there, Harney!" she called. "Drop your rifle and put up your hands!"

Harney's head tilted upward at Jessie's first words, and he stopped in his tracks when he saw her in the open window with her rifle shouldered. He'd been carrying his rifle in his left hand, and now he raised his arm and held his weapon away from his body, his arm extended full-length.

Jessie was waiting for the swindler to obey her command and drop the weapon when Bettina Van Horn ran out of the building and started toward Harney.

"Oh, Mr. Harney!" she called as she ran. "Don't start shooting! I don't want anybody to be killed!"

In spite of her concentration on Harney, Bettina's sudden appearance and her shout to Harney distracted Jessie's attention. She let the rifle muzzle drop only a fraction of an inch, but it was not on target when Harney suddenly moved.

Using one of the oldest tricks in a shootist's book, the swindler flipped up the butt of his rifle, and his right hand darted forward with the speed of a striking rattlesnake to grasp the weapon at the throat of the stock as his forefinger sought the trigger.

Jessie's response was instinctive, but it was backed by the skill she'd acquired through reactions finely honed in similar instants of crisis. She lifted the rifle an inch as her finger squeezed off her shot. Before the slug from Harney's weapon splintered the windowsill beside her, the bullet from the Winchester plowed into Harney, and at almost the same instant one of Ki's *shuriken* flashed through the air and sliced into the swindler's head.

Harney was already crumpling from the impact of Jessie's slug when the *shuriken* tore into his brain. His arms sagged and his knees buckled. The muzzle of his rifle dropped to touch the ground before his lifeless body lurched forward and lay sprawled over the useless weapon.

Ki had risen to his feet to launch the *shuriken* and had seen Jessie flinch instinctively as Harney's rifle bullet tore chips of wood from the windowframe.

"Jessie?" he called. "Are you all right?"

"Don't worry, Ki," she replied. "I'm fine!"

"That's good," Ki called back. "Now, do you want me to bring Harney's body down there to the house, or shall I get Van Horn to give me a hand bringing it in later?"

"Later, I think," Jessie said. "We can load it on their wagon and save you having to carry it."

"That's a better idea," Ki answered. "I'll come on in,

then, and we can look over Harney's papers while there's still plenty of light."

Jessie wasted no time hurrying down the stairs and to the outer door. Bettina was still standing just outside the door, her eyes glazed, her jaw sagging. Jessie slapped her face with her open palm. Bettina came out of her trance slowly, blinking her eyes as though she was still half-dazed.

"Where's Nelius?" she asked. "I want him to take me out of this terrible place as fast as we can move!"

"I'm right here, Bettina," Cornelius said from the doorway behind Jessie. "And I'm as ready to go as you are. Go pack now, while I hitch up the wagon. It'll only take me a few minutes."

Jessie turned when Cornelius spoke and, as he walked away, saw Matt Bolton standing behind him in the doorway. She asked, "Are you all right, Matt?"

"Better'n I've got any right to be, I guess," Bolton told her. "I'm sorry I couldn't help you more."

"That's not your fault," Jessie said. "You tried. And if you're still interested in the timber rights to this property, I'd be glad to work out an agreement with you before we leave."

"You're going back to San Francisco, I guess?"

"We'll leave here tomorrow or next day and spend a few days there," Jessie said. "But as soon as our business is finished we'll be heading back to Texas."

"Then I better get down to my own place and make sure the boys are still working. But I'll be back tomorrow to talk to you about the timber lease."

Ki came up just as Bolton was walking away. "I suppose we have the job of burying Harney," he said.

"It looks that way," Jessie said, nodding. Before she could say anything more Cornelius Van Horn drove up in the wagon. Jessie went on, "Unless Cornelius wants to stay here long enough to give us a hand."

"A hand at what?" Van Horn asked.

"Burying Clem Harney," Jessie replied. "We can't just leave him laying out there in the meadow."

Before Van Horn could reply there was a thud behind Jessie, and she turned to see Bettina standing beside the suitcase she'd just dropped.

"Now, don't you say a word, Nelius," Bettina snapped. "Let me handle this!" Turning to Jessie, she went on, "We are leaving here this minute, Jessie, to go back home. It isn't that we have anything against you, and you're welcome to visit at our home any time. But Cornelius will not stay and help you with such a gruesome task! I suppose living on that ranch way out in Texas the way you do, you're used to a rougher kind of life than I am, if you don't mind my saying so."

"Perhaps you're right, Bettina," Jessie agreed, anxious now to get rid of the pair. She looked at Ki and said, "We'll just have to bury Clem Harney out in the meadow, then."

"We can do that, of course," Ki said. "And I'm sure Cornelius and Bettina will have time while they're waiting for their train to notify the sheriff of what's happened. He may want to come up here and investigate the killing."

"We'll be glad to do that, Jessie," Van Horn said quickly, before Bettina could object. Then, turning to his wife, he went on, "Now, it'll only take us a few minutes, and we'll have to wait for the night train in Truckee anyhow."

"We can't leave too soon to suit me," Bettina replied. She looked at Harney's body lying sprawled in the meadow and then said to Jessie, "I don't see how you can endure it. But I guess the things you have to do on that ranch in Texas—"

"Aren't all pleasant," Jessie broke in. "That's why not everybody can get accustomed to ranching, Bettina. It takes some people too close to the realities of life and death. Now, if you and Cornelius are going to get to Truckee today, you'd better get started."

"Yes, we had," Van Horn agreed. "And remember that Bettina and I will welcome a visit from you on your way home, if you care to stop."

"Oh, certainly," Bettina nodded, her voice anything but enthusiastic. "But as you said, Jessie, we really must be on our way."

For a moment Jessie and Ki stood gazing at the spring wagon as it rolled down the vestigial trail leading to the Truckee road. Then she turned to Ki.

"I think Bettina must still be in a state of shock. Now, let's get this unpleasant job finished before dark, Ki. I have a hunch that when we start going through Clem Harney's safe, we're going to find enough of his crooked work to undo to keep us busy the rest of the night."